M000006150

The King of Vermont

Also by Stephen Morris

Beyond Yonder
The Great Beer Trek
The Book of Heat (with William Busha)

The King of Vermont

Vermont

Stephen Morris

William Morrow and Company, Inc. / New York

Library of Congress Cataloging-in-Publication Data

Morris, Stephen, 1948-
    The king of Vermont / Stephen Morris.
       p.   cm.
    ISBN 0-688-08428-1
    I. Title.
    PS3563.0874477K56   1989
    813'.54—dc19   89-2868
                                                                                      CIP

Printed in the United States of America

First Edition

1 2 3 4 5 6 7 8 9 10

BOOK DESIGN BY BRIAN MOLLOY

Here's to the women who create the men who oppress the women.

—from Darwin Hunter's favorite drinking toast

Preface

The Lifeboat Theory

When is a lifeboat full? Exactly one second after you get on board. A similar mentality afflicts the people of the northland, each of whom has secured a spot on the lifeboat. That's it! That's enough. Let's cast off before we are scuttled by the raging herd. Best that some survive, rather than that we all perish.

Once adrift, the lifeboat provides its own arena, a stage, albeit small, upon which life's dramas can be played. The dramas do not get much smaller than those of Upper Granville, Vermont, the mythical setting for this book, as well the previously published *Beyond Yonder*. In that book the scenes concerned the confrontations of those with secure positions on the lifeboat (called Chucks) and others (Flatlanders) who were noisily splashing aboard. This time the focus is even narrower, as if the microscope has been clicked up a notch in power.

Several people contributed strongly to the creation of

this book. My wife, Laura, has supported my efforts in more ways than can be acknowledged here. Sons Jake and Patrick have indulged a father who spends too much time staring at a gray screen with green letters when he could be playing computer games or flipping baseball cards.

Maryjane Kennedy and Don Hooper gave me two dedicated and able readers. Maryjane's eye and ear for native tongue and custom saved me from many an embarrassing clang, while Don's knowledge of the mechanics of state government provided essential guidance for a political neophyte. I am thankful that Don, as a hardworking farmer, entrepreneur, and state representative, found the energy to help with this project.

My editors at William Morrow, Doug Stumpf and Jared Stamm, cut out (in my opinion) all of the funniest lines from the manuscript, and, in doing so, saved an author from embarrassing self-indulgence. There is room on the lifeboat for all of you.

1

Straddlin' the Fence

Riley Gore's hair was perfect. And still, the self-proclaimed Gray Fox of the Green Mountains dabbed frantically with licked fingertips at immaculate sideburns as technicians scurried in preparation for the weekly broadcast of Channel 5's local feature show, *Straddlin' the Fence*. His guest, Darwin Hunter of Upper Granville, Vermont, sat silently, blood pounding in his head from a necktie drawn too tight.

Gore sat in a chair shaped like a giant human hand. Darwin sank into a new, overly soft couch. Behind them was a backdrop of plastic plants and a veneered bookcase filled with random titles purchased at a yard sale. The rest of the studio was empty, save for the lights, wires, cameras, and operators.

"What question will you ask first?" Darwin spoke to break the tension as well as to make sure that all frogs were cleared from his throat. Gore paid as much attention to Darwin's question as does a cow to a fly on its butt. Instead, he stared at Hunter as he would at a mirror.

"Are my brows all right?" he asked with genuine curiosity, smoothing them with four quick flicks.

"Your brows are perfect," returned Hunter.

"You've got a goober, right here," Gore reached over and brushed a spot just right and center of Darwin's lip. Nothing happened. "Guess it's a freckle," sighed Gore.

"Ten seconds, R.G., theme music up," said the cameraman, touching his headset. Gore's visage froze in a wide smile. The camera responded by transforming his high blood pressure into ruddy healthfulness. Hunter clasped his hands so tightly that the fingertips turned white. He imagined blood draining from his brain, a loss of consciousness, and a spastic pitch forward into his host's lap.

"Five, four, three, two . . . we're live."

Gore's transformation was complete. This was no longer a vain, little man, but rather the ol' Vermonter himself, the Gray Fox of the Green Mountains:

"Hello, hello, neighbors. Howdy-hi, and welcome to another edition of *Straddlin' the Fence*, Vermont's show of what's new and, well, what's just plain interesting. I'm Riley Gore and my guest tonight is an interesting fella who has written a book about a little place that's as Vermont as I am, Upper Granville. His name is, uh, Durwood Huntoon. Welcome to *Straddlin' the Fence*."

Gore showed his teeth for a nanosecond, then continued: "Durwood, your neighbors must hate you. Vermonters don't like people splattering their private lives on the pages of a book."

"Well, Riley," Darwin replied, trying to match Gore's geniality, "Upper Granville isn't exactly Peyton Place. I think my neighbors liked the book."

"All of them?"

"I didn't do a survey."

"So maybe some of them didn't like it, and thought it was an exploitive piece of trash."

"I suppose it's possible."

Gore's ruddy face tightened into a knowing smirk. He nodded like a rowboat bobbing at the dock. His eyes darted about quickly to determine which camera was on. He addressed it directly:

"Not just possible, Mr. Hartly, but inevitable. You'll understand when you get to know Vermonters like the old Gray Fox knows Vermonters."

After a full eight seconds of camera nodding, he continued: "I understand you're not a writer, but, of all things, a doctor. Well, not a real doctor, but an eye doctor. What does reading eye charts have to do with writing a book?"

Darwin chuckled, struggling to remain unflustered. No sense getting bent out of shape over Riley Gore's medical ignorance. "Actually, I am a real doctor—an ophthalmologist, in fact."

"Can you prescribe glasses?"

"Of course, but an optometrist—"

"Good," the Gray Fox turned directly to the camera, "because the last time I read the newspaper I realized I needed either new glasses or a longer arm."

Gore guffawed for several seconds, prolonging the mirth until his guest managed a twisted smile. Then he launched into an anecdote about a doctor who treated all ailments with bag balm, the miracle ointment for cow udders. This, in turn, segued into an exposition of the host's views on socialized medicine, only after which did the interview resume:

"But seriously, Derwin, where did you get the idea to write a book, and what's it all about?"

At last! A question Darwin had anticipated. He had answered it repeatedly while lying in bed, while riding in the car, and while staring blankly out his office window. He had honed his response by practicing on children. He wrote it down; he revised and edited it. In less than one minute he could tell about the town of Upper Granville and how it became the unlikely meeting ground for two opposing factions of rural life: the native Chucks and the invading Flatlanders. He could wax eloquent on the history of this tiny hamlet, crediting Alton Blanchard's minor, yet poignant, masterpiece, *Over Yonder Hill*, the book that had inspired him. From there he might nimbly tiptoe into a lighthearted yet incisive examination of the contemporary juxtaposition of sharply contrasting lifestyles that formed the foundation of his sequel to Alton's book, *Beyond Yonder*.

"I'm glad you asked that, Riley," began Darwin, brimming with confidence and with a cocky lilt to his voice. "Upper Granville is really a unique place."

"One of the many in Vermont," interjected Gore. "In fact, it reminds me of Sussex Junction, where I live."

The truth was, Gore had scarcely set foot in Sussex Junction for the last five years, but spent most of his time in a modern Burlington condominium with a twenty-three-year-old mistress. But he regarded the town of Sussex Junction as an integral part of his public persona, as much as the ruddy complexion and gray hair, and Darwin had committed a lethal error by opening the gate to the fertile field of Gore's personal mythology. Gore prattled on for five minutes about the idiosyncracies of his alleged hometown with its roster of colorful (and invented) characters —the one-legged storekeeper who provided instant profundity on any topic, the lady postmaster who minded everyone's business but the U.S. government's, and the likable, but hopelessly impractical, urban refugees from Perth Amboy, New Jersey (coincidentally, Gore's real hometown).

Darwin sat politely and feigned interest, sporting an expression of beatific bemusement, but knowing well that his hope for fame and fortune was slipping down the toilet.

Eventually Gore chortled his way back to Darwin's book: "So your book concerns the age-old rivalry between the so-called Chucks, short for 'woodchucks,' and the so-called Flatlanders? Frankly, in my humble opinion—and what do I know, I'm just the Gray Fox of the Green Mountains—this is a subject that we have heard too much of lately. Don't you agree, Durwin, that instead of focusing on the differences between these groups we should emphasize their similarities?"

The final "Durwin" pushed Darwin over the invisible line that demarcated animal from civilized behavior. His reply was growled from a curled upper lip:

"If I thought that, then I wouldn't have spent six years writing the book, would I, R.G.? Or should I call you 'Foxy'?"

Gore tried to parry his guest's sarcasm. "Say, you know, there's an interesting story about how I got that name. Now the gray fox is quite rare in Vermont. Mostly—"

"Oh, go fox yourself!" interrupted Hunter, locking on to his prey. "Let me ask you a question. Did you even read my book? Did you even look at the pictures? Can you read?"

Gore blustered about his meticulous preparation for each show. He reviewed his academic background, lying about a college degree from Harvard, and implied he was briefed daily by a crack research team. Hunter, however, never let the wounded prey from his sights.

"Did . . . you . . . read . . . the . . . book?"

Gore looked to the technicians for help. He intimidated the quilters and cloggers who comprised the normal fare for *Straddlin' the Fence*. This guy, however, was not falling into place.

"Hey, whose show is this anyway?" he managed weakly. No one in the crew broke stride. Riley realized that he was out there, alone in television land. He launched back into his tried-and-true smile. "Well, Durwood. We're running low on time. With one successful book and a career as an optometrist behind you, what's next? Another book?"

Darwin fixed on to Gore a ten-second stare that, translated into action, was the equivalent of World War III. Riley's blood drained from his face. Finally, Darwin broke the stalemate:

"No, Riley. I'm sick of writing books. I've decided to go into politics."

"Politics," Gore babbled. "Now there's a field where it pays to have good eyesight." He giggled. Darwin glowered. Gore spoke: "What are you running for?"

"King," mumbled Darwin, trying his best to sound like Marlon Brando during his young-buck period.

"King! Oh, this is rich, and you heard it first on *Straddlin' the Fence*. King of what?"

"King of the World, well, King of Vermont, anyway."

"And what will your kingdom be like?"

"No plague, no pestilence, no acid rain, no insipid talk show hosts. Do you know what the penalty will be in my kingdom for a talk show host not reading a guest's book?"

"What?"

"We'll cut his tongue off."

Gore heh-heh-heh'd for a moment, then made a comment about how good vision and a sense of humor made an unbeatable combination in the political arena. Suddenly his face brightened, as if he had just guessed the punchline of a good joke.

"I get it. Now, I get it." One of the crew held up a sign that read ONE MINUTE.

"Politics and show business make strange bedfellows, eh, Huntoon?" Gore's voice contained both a nudge and a wink. "Write a little book. Get yourself on Vermont's most controversial television talk show, and then announce your candidacy to run for the Fifth District Senate seat currently held by Linwood 'Woody' Dunwoody."

Gore paused for dramatic effect, as if he expected someone to proclaim "good boy!" and to scratch him behind the ears.

"Yeah," conceded Hunter with an air of resignation, as if Jessica Fletcher had just named him the culprit. "You saw right through me. You knew what I was after all along."

THIRTY SECONDS, read the card held up by the stagehand.

"You had me going for a minute," said Riley, now grinning like a Cheshire cat. He turned to face the camera and his public. "You've heard it first on *Straddlin' the Fence*, a surprise announcement for the Senate seat from the Fifth District. It should be a great campaign, one that we'll keep you abreast of as we approach election time. Our guest tonight has been eye doctor, author, and, I'll tell ya, a guy with a unique sense of humor, Darren Huntly. We'll be seeing you next week on *Straddlin' the Fence*. Until then, byedy-bye."

* * *

Darwin Hunter, forty years old, whippet thin, with a receding sandy hairline, climbed into his silver Saab Turbo, and drove approximately two hundred yards from the Channel 5 studios to Manny and Marie's Quik-Stop, where he bought a six-pack of Miller Lite beer. Upon returning to the car, he discovered that he had locked himself out. Only after an expletive (Shit!) and a kicked driver's-side door did he remember that he could crawl in through the hatchback.

Darwin fumed generally at the world. He fumed at his car. He had bought himself a silver Saab Turbo every other year for the better part of a decade, and could not believe what a vehicular dullard he had become. "My next car," he vowed swinging onto the northbound on-ramp for Interstate 89, "is a Yugo. Guaranteed. Three thousand nine hundred ninety-five bucks, and I won't pay a nickel more. I don't want style, I don't want identity, I don't want status, I just want to go."

He ruminated deeply on cars. Only when he saw the sign for the Canadian border did he realize he was heading in the wrong direction. "You asshole," he said softly to no one, and felt better.

Heading south and with the first beer under his belt, Darwin's mood softened. "I'm really a lucky guy," he told himself. How could he take a half-wit like Gore seriously? He had watched the insipid interviews on *Straddlin' the Fence* many times; why had he expected the Gray Fox of the Green Mountains to suddenly become William Buckley? And why did he go off on the tangent about being King of Vermont?

Still, he felt depressed. What had he accomplished in his forty years? What did it mean? With the cruise control at sixty-five mph and the Winooski River twisting along-side, Darwin, in between his second and third beer, turned contemplative.

There was a book, *Over Yonder Hill*, by Alton Blanchard, that chronicled the rise and decline of Upper Granville, Vermont, from the period 1768–1969. Although fewer than a thousand copies were printed, Darwin Hunter, who moved to Upper Granville in 1979, found something in it of lasting significance.

The Upper Granville that Alton left, both in his book and at the time of his self-inflicted death, was on the brink of extinction. The schoolhouse was closed, the farms con-solidated. Houses lay vacant; grass grew on the center strip of the dirt road. Then came the "back to the land" move-ment. Refugees from the suburban Flatlands saw beauty in decaying farmhouses. *Country Journal* became a bible, home canning a sacrament. Animal husbandry was seen as recreation, and Garrison Keillor was Johnny Carson and God rolled into one.

The movement was not without conflict. In fact, one might say that conflict was its outstanding single charac-teristic. The newcomers' often misguided enthusiasm for rural craft was perceived by native Vermonters as excessive and condescending. Indeed, the Vermonters observed their new neighbors with both bemusement and scorn. True, they were revitalizing the neighborhood, but in the process, instilling it with values light-years away from tra-ditional priorities of rural life. Yes, the property was im-proved, but at prices so high that the only possible buyers were other Flatlanders.

Such was the world of *Beyond Yonder*. Darwin under-took this sequel as a labor of love, an attempt to portray a sliver of Americana. Reaction to the book was similar to that elicited by a group photo. Great portrait, said each individual, except you snapped the shutter when my eyes were closed. The camera tells the truth for everyone but me.

This reaction was good enough for Darwin. What was significant about *Beyond Yonder*, he knew, was not its depiction of life in a Central Vermont hamlet, but rather its microcosmic summary of the most salient issues of twentieth-century life. Here was Man, the social being, encountering his own frailties within a pristine laboratory of the Northwoods. Here was Life, without the streaky mud of the material world; a chance to glimpse the aboriginal state of the human species.

These were the points Darwin had intended to make to Riley Gore, not to mention the world. *Beyond Yonder* was more than a collection of neo-rural homilies; it was Life, it was Art, it was . . .

Darwin checked himself as he turned onto the off-ramp. *Beyond Yonder* was, to be honest, a small book by an amateur author with so narrow an appeal that not even a mental midget of Rileyesque dimension could be bothered reading it.

Before turning onto the dirt road leading from Route 100 to Upper Granville, Darwin stopped at the Granville General Store. Its new owner, Howard Pease, was a refugee from Hewlett-Packard. He brought to the store an encyclopedic knowledge on every subject known to man as well as an obsession to overanalyze every aspect of his business. Howard (dubbed "Warren" by Darwin) had replaced the insightful homilies of the late Oakley McBean, the store's former proprietor, with pages of analysis from his Macintosh computer, to show the return per square foot of every item in the store. But despite the changes of style and proprietor, the role of the store as community gossip center remained intact. It was the need for gossip, not merchandise, that drew Darwin. Warren sat alone and motionless at the cash register. Below the counter the black and white, nine-inch television droned.

"If it ain't the TV star, Durwood Huntoon," drawled Warren.

"Hey, that's good, Warren. I bet you didn't say ain't back when you were with H-P."

"That's true, but we used to say What if? a helluva lot."

"You're my first official review. How was I?"

"Silent, mostly. That Riley Gore didn't give you much daylight. You looked ready to punch his lights out."

"The guy is a vain, supercilious maggot."

Warren sucked on an unlit pipe. He was trying to learn to smoke so as to better affect the image of a rural pundit. He was far from mastering the craft:

"You really got him with that King of Vermont routine."

"How did it come across?"

"Like you meant business."

"Good. Am I a star?"

"No, but the real question is 'are you a candidate?' "

From the store Darwin drove up the dirt road toward Upper Granville. At the peak of the hill there was a hole in the foliage that permitted a panoramic view of the town. He cut the engine, grabbed an unopened beer, and climbed out to survey the scene. The twilight of August lit the west-facing hills. Summer was still in full sway, although the intensity of green had been slowly sucked back into the roots of the trees, and an occasional slash of red foretold autumn.

The summer had been dry. The spring that fed the Cowdrey House, home to valley transients, had gone dry, necessitating that the current occupant, Gimp Fenvessey, a one-armed freelance journalist, fill up two plastic gallon jugs at the Hunters' each morning. It had also necessitated that the owner of the Cowdrey House, Walt Gunion, ace local realtor/entrepreneur, bite the bullet and invest in a drilled well. The drilling rig was there now. A hundred twenty feet, and still no water.

The Gunion place was perched on a hillside to the north. It, too, had been affected by the drought. The mud hole that Walt and Martha called a pond was now an unabashed slime puddle ringed by oxygen-deprived fish.

Darwin could see his children playing kickball with the Clarke kids and Bobby Pisano, who had become the neighborhood juvenile delinquent. Right now they were all yelling at General Beauregard, the Hunters' golden retriever, who had wandered onto the field of play. In less than two weeks they would start school once again. He could also see that the agricultural-industrial complex of the Blanchard Farm was in high gear, as the mop-up campaign on the second cutting neared completion. The patriarch, Hoyt, drove the baler, while their farmhand, Emil Dummerston Weed, raced back and forth to the barn, pulling the hay wagon behind the John Deere. Bennett was nowhere to be seen, but was likely stacking the bales in the barn.

The smell right now was green and lazy. Tomorrow they would let the cows into the fields to munch on the late summer growth. Then came the siege of manure, taking them almost to the first snow.

Darwin sipped his beer. He saw Hannah Duncan, sixty-one years old and thin as a bean, padding in her running shoes, getting ready to whip Darwin's ass in the annual 'round-the-valley race. There was Teresa Blanchard's pink Chevette, the proud steed of a determined Mary Kay Cosmetics fledgling. There was Joe Pisano's satellite dish. Old Joe was probably sitting in front of the tube right now, thought Darwin, watching a Portuguese soccer match or reruns of *Leave It to Beaver*. And there was Darwin's own home, a brick Federal standing tall, the one-time community tavern. Just west was the Blanchard farmhouse, including the doublewide where the next generation— Bennett and Teresa—awaited their turns at the big house.

Contentment overwhelmed Darwin Hunter. "Not so bad," he said to the trees, and returned to his car.

The community had changed since its depiction in *Beyond Yonder*. Darwin thought it to be in a holding pattern, perhaps like an adolescent on the verge of a growth spurt. But, for all its nuances, Upper Granville was marked less by change than constants—the relentless winters, the creeping hardwood forest, the inspiration of fiery leaves, the agony of midwinter thaws, and the Blanchards.

The Blanchards, who counted Alton, author of *Over Yonder Hill*, among their members, had dominated the high valley since the early 1800s, when Hiram, the original Blanchard, migrated southward from Baddeck, Nova Scotia. The current patriarch was Hoyt Blanchard, a barrel-chested workhorse who had "retired" to mere twelve-hour workdays to spend more time smelling the sweet peas (roses don't do very well in Vermont). Hoyt was aided and abetted by the spindly Stella Blanchard, who came to the valley as the schoolmarm and who now reigned as queen mother.

Within the Blanchard clan both Stella and her daughter-in-law Teresa championed *Beyond Yonder*. The ex-teacher in Stella compelled her to encourage any pretensions of the creation of literature or the recording of history. Teresa Blanchard spent several anxious months wondering if Darwin's book would reveal their misguided night of shared lust in the parking lot of the Tunbridge World's Fair. When she saw their secret protected, she became *Beyond Yonder*'s biggest booster, interpreting the book as a glorification of the Blanchard clan. Darwin might have been a transient, as native Vermonters regarded all newcomers, but at least he perceived the nobility of the family farm.

The male Blanchards disdained the book, failing to see the point to any venture that did not have as its focus the pulling of cow teats. On the other hand, Emil Dummerston Weed, the Blanchard farmhand and Woodchuck extraordinaire, found the lampooning of Flatlander frailty hilarious. "Only thing dummer'n a turkey is a Flatlander, and Darwin put it in black and white," he snorted. The significant events in Emil's life revolved around the price of Genesee beer (now over three bucks a six-pack) and the fate of the Boston Red Sox (eleven games out with only five weeks of the season left).

Darwin took mental stock of the status of his beloved community. The Pisanos, Joe and Tina, were reasonably intact. Two children, one whose hormones were beginning to run wild. Joe's plumbing and heating business had prospered—money for a new truck, the satellite dish, and all the beer he cared to drink. It don't get no better than this. His wife Tina was firmly entrenched in her mid-life crisis, recovering her flat stomach via hours of aerobics and Jazz-ercize classes.

Darwin scanned the village. There had been casualties, to be sure. The Stowe Stallion, the self-appointed vigilante of architectural propriety, had taken his preservation act to Manhattan. His lovingly restored cape stood vacant, its future unknown.

B. J. Bosco, Darwin's partner as the photographer of *Beyond Yonder*, was reportedly the owner of a crab shack and shrimp boat somewhere on the Redneck Riviera of Florida. Her place had been admirably yet not fully filled by Hannah Duncan, who stood defiant against the world, having outlasted three husbands.

As for the children: three Hunters, two Clarkes, two Pisanos, four Blanchards. Lots of Lamaze had gone over the bridge. Now the last of the offspring had reached the school-bus stage, and the moms were returning to the world with a vengeance. Townshend Clarke, Darwin's closest neighbor, had weathered repeated identity crises, his wife Sue an affair, Darwin a book, and Sammi Berger-Hunter, Darwin. Life within the families, Darwin had to admit, was contentious. This, he assumed, was normal.

Darwin swung into the driveway, the telltale whine of the Saab absorbed by the surrounding hills. He paused in the front yard. The kickball game was over and the kids were rooted by the television. The green hillsides were careening toward summer darkness. He scanned the close horizons, then peed. "My turf," he said. Incandescent light streamed from the Hunter household, the travelers' wayside. Inside, the wood stove stood at the ready, the children were safe, and his wife Sammi was probably reading some feminist novel. Comforts awaited him—his display of rock-and-roll memorabilia, his collection of single malt Scotches, the dog-eared copies of *Over Yonder Hill* and *Beyond Yonder*. Riley Gore, and the overwhelming artificiality of the television studio, seemed far, far away.

General Beauregard, his loyal but increasingly ancient

golden retriever, thumped a welcome with his tail on the front porch. He tapped out a message that said, "Glad to see you, Master. I'd get up, but you know how it is when you get to my age. By the way, you really did a number on the Gray Fox today."

Darwin, of course, understood. He spent a minute scratching the General.

"Just think," he murmured, "you'll be the Royal Hound."

He looked in through the window onto a tableau of tranquility. His wife, Sammi, sat engrossed in a book. She was still dressed in flowered Lycra tights that she wore to the Jazz-ercize class she took twice a week in Montpelier. Darwin opened the door and fired off a good-natured reference to her young, muscle-bound instructor:

"So how're Georgio's deltoids today?"

"It's 'Gregorio,' not Georgio. And you've been drinking."

"Amazing," answered her husband. "You don't even have to look up from your book to criticize me."

"You promised not to drink and drive."

"I promised not to drive drunk. I have had three, count the empties if you'd like, Miller Lites. Each contains roughly twelve grams of ethanol. For a one-hundred-sixty-pound man to be legally drunk, his blood must contain a minimum of point one percent alcohol. Translated into layman's—excuse me, lay person's—terms, this means eight or nine beers. Except this is mitigated by the fact that the body dissipates the equivalent of one drink an hour, so—"

"Stop rationalizing. You're a drunk."

"Not according to the law."

"And you're a fool."

"Aha, perhaps the real reason for this attack will now be revealed."

Sammi wore half glasses for reading, and she shifted them lower on her nose, as if to emphasize her disdain.

"Darwin, how could you?" she began.

"How could I drink three Miller Lites?"

"And stop your infernal wiseass answers. How could you make such a fool of us tonight?"

"Us, white man? I thought I made a fool of Riley Gore."

"Goddamn you!" Sammi hurled the book, a hardbound copy of Toni Morrison's *Beloved*, at Darwin's head. He ducked and the book smashed a pane on one of the twelve-over-twelve windows in the Hunter kitchen. Darwin made no move to clean up the mess, but simply picked up the book and sat down at a chair he pulled from the kitchen table.

"I had a tough time getting into this book," he said.

"That doesn't surprise me."

"Why not?"

"You're not a woman; you're not black; and you're not sensitive."

"Well, I can read," he said calmly. "Maybe you can explain to me the source of what appears to be gratuitous hostility?"

"You know that I've been auditing courses at the law school. You know that my favorite course, 'The Legal Woman,' is taught by Natalie Weinstein. And Natalie Weinstein has been widely touted as the Democratic candidate for the Senate race in the Fifth District. She's qualified, she's serious, she's committed. She's everything you are not. And you have to go on television and make a big joke of the whole thing."

"The only thing I made a joke of was Riley Gore."

Sammi's eyes were ablaze. "You made a joke of yourself, but I don't know why you had to drag Natalie Weinstein and me down with you."

"Do you want to hear my side of this? Or does it make you happier to fuss and fume? First, I've never heard of Natalie Weinstein. Second—"

"She's perfect to represent our district, but she needs all the help she can get to run that political hack Linwood 'Woody' Dunwoody out of office. She doesn't need a dink like you making cheap jokes on television about the campaign."

"A dink? You called me a dink?" Darwin's face contorted in disgust.

"There are no words bad enough for you, Darwin. Everything is a joke to you. People's lives are a joke. The government is a joke. Society's a joke. Your whole life is the pursuit of cheap thrills, and I'm sick of it. Just leave Natalie Weinstein, and me, out of it."

Darwin was still preoccupied. "A dink. From a king to a dink in less than two hours. After sixteen years of marriage I had hoped for something with a little more substance. Maybe 'bahstahrd!' or 'sunuvabitch!' or even 'scumbag.' But 'dink' is really low rent." He stood up and prepared his exit.

Sammi had a final salvo: " 'Dink' is about the size of it. You're not enough of a villain for those other words. You're just a forty-year-old man going on fourteen. You're too much of a coward to face your own feelings, so you hide behind your snide little witticisms and snicker at any reference to big boobs."

Darwin remained undaunted. "Luckily, there are thousands of dinks in the world. They all have votes, and they are crying for leadership. That leadership cannot be provided by reactionary political hacks like Dunwoody, or bleeding-heart liberals like Weinstein. They want a dink in their own image."

"You're not serious?" said Sammi, eyes widening to full moons. "You think you have a prayer against pros like Dunwoody and Weinstein? Why don't you just go to bed, and in the morning this will all seem like a confused dream from your alcohol-ridden, adolescent mind."

Darwin turned, aiming for the sanctity of his den. He paused before passing through the doorway, considering the appropriate closing zinger. He thought better, continued, then whirled back into the kitchen. For the second time this day he had been provoked to reach deep into his animal self. His tongue became leather, his teeth yellow, his mouth a cavern of dry salt. He spit the words out slowly, one by one, each a gritty morsel of bone:

"I'm gonna run. And I'm gonna win." Darwin narrowed his eyes to look like Clint Eastwood facing down six guns in the Mexican sun, "And I'm gonna kick butt."

2

A Plague of Voyagers

Darwin had not yet settled into his desk chair before Sammi reached her best friend Sue Clarke on the phone. She projected her voice so that he could hear every syllable, her sentences truncated by spasms of hilarity:

"So he wheels around, with the skin all tight on his face. I thought maybe he was having a heart attack. And then he—he—he says, completely serious—Oh, you're not going to believe this. *You're not going to believe this!* I can't even say it." Her words, choked by mirth, hit Darwin like small, bony fists. Finally she regained composure:

"He says, 'I'm gonna—' Oh, I can't say it. He says, 'I'm gonna win, and I'm gonna kick butt.' "

Darwin poured himself two fingers of Laphroaig, a delightfully smoky single-malt Scotch from the Isle of Islay. Sammi finished with Sue, referring to him as Mr. Kick Butt, and placed a second call.

"Don't forget to call your mother," called Darwin from his sanctuary.

Within forty-five minutes most people in Central Vermont would know of Darwin's pronouncement. Sammi even made sure that Martha Gunion included it in the community news for the Granville *Clarion*. There it was, right after Tina Pisano's parents visiting from Somerville, Massachusetts, and Hoyt Blanchard's squash shaped like the space shuttle.

> Upper Granville's own Darwin Hunter, who proclaimed himself King of Vermont last week on *Straddlin' the Fence*, reports that Riley Gore is just as warm and genuine in person as he is on television. According to Darwin's wife, Sammi, he will be "kicking butt" in this year's senatorial race.

For a period of three weeks, until the first blast of arctic air blew into town, its sterile chill slapping everyone back to reality, "kicking butt" superseded the reopening of school, the turning of the leaves, and even the Tunbridge World's Fair as a topic of local interest. When Darwin went running, Emil Dummerston Weed, from the seat of his John Deere, embellished a wave with a "There goes Mr. Kick Butt himself." Darwin answered the phone with his usual hello, only to hear Tina Pisano ask whether he'd kicked any butt as yet that day. Townshend called him "the ol' Butt Kicker," and a casual comment on the weather to Howard "Warren" Pease at the Granville General Store brought the retort, "Perfect day for kicking butt." Even his eldest son, Duke, was in on the act, referring to him across the dinner table as Captain Kick Butt.

Darwin did not bother to reply, but retreated gracefully to his study for nightly rumination. The ridicule, stemming from Sammi and the *Clarion*'s comments, he knew, was his wife's way of avoiding the conflict inherent in their lives. The dilemma was simple enough. Both were poised at crossroads, the brink of middle age. Darwin was in love with the way they lived, and felt that future progress could be built upon the existing foundation. Change must come from within.

Sammi had emerged on the other side of three children, needing to make up for lost time. Upper Granville and Darwin's complacency stood in the way, and were, therefore, the enemies. She was stuck in the middle of nowhere. Jazz-ercize, mail order catalogues, and her law courses were lifelines to a whole person, and she clung to them as tenaciously as Darwin and the children clung to her.

A million times he tried to tell her, "Honey, you're doing great," and a million times she replied, "That's easy for you to say."

With the exception of his wife's pointed barbs, the butt-kicker comments were good-humored retaliation at a guy who was a fair target for gibes, needles, and ridicule. Any extrovert who leads with his chin must be able to take the occasional punch. For the moment, figured Darwin, it was his turn to take. This was the man who stuck plastic flamingos in the front yard of an old brick tavern in a classic Vermont village, the doctor who counted among his most prized possessions a twisted hunk of fuselage from the plane that went down with Buddy Holly, the forty-year-old who was constantly reprimanded by his eight-year-old to grow up.

"Admit it," said Darwin to the loyal General Beauregard, who joined him for his nightly ruminations in his study, "I'm a good target. I'm the straw that stirs the drink, a Reggie Jackson of the North. People love to see me hit home runs, but they like it even more when the ball rolls through my legs."

Darwin's stirring began as soon as he moved to Upper Granville in the late 1970s. An uninhibited suburban refugee, he broke through centuries of calcified Yankee inhibition. Before long the Chucks and Flatlanders, whose contact had been polite nods and waves, linked by occasional platitudes about the weather, confronted each other openly. And somehow, amid the pettiness, human bonds were formed.

This world was rent asunder with the departures of community stalwarts Bruce "the Stowe Stallion" Liebermann and B. J. Bosco, not to mention the untimely death of the venerable storekeeper Oakley McBean. Some, including Sammi, felt the community had lost its critical mass and would revert to the mossy Appalachian backwater depicted by Alton Blanchard. Darwin responded by redoubling efforts to keep the community vital. Repeatedly he sought the common chord to unify Upper Granville. Like a determined spider he tried, tried again and again, never looking back at the futility of previous efforts. Now, at night in his study, he leafed through the great ideas he had inflicted upon his neighbors to get a sense of his overall contribution.

The Upper Granville Investment Club

The idea was simple enough. As the neighborhood residents collectively approached middle age, they could plan for the future by setting aside a modest sum of money (twenty-five dollars) on a monthly basis, then meet periodically (quarterly) to discuss how best to manage it.

Everyone warmed to the idea. Even dairy farmers get

old. Each individual was allowed fifteen minutes for an investment proposal. They ranged from Bennett Blanchard's well-researched plan to purchase a wood lot that promised capital appreciation, as well as a tangible return on investment in the form of firewood, to Gimp Fenvessey's harebrained scheme idea to go to Atlantic City to drop the wad on double zero.

Joe Pisano had a different idea, however. The group could earn a handsome return of two percent above prime by purchasing a new panel van for Pisano's Plumbing and Heating which he, in turn, would pay for in installments. "In other words," snorted Bennett, "we get to buy you a new truck."

It was Howard "Warren" Pease in whom they ultimately placed their trust. Warren used his ample spare time and sophisticated Macintosh computer to perform detailed ratio analyses on more than one thousand common stocks. Finally, he found one listed on the penny stock exchange in Denver that fit all criteria. It was something everyone could live with morally. It offered terrific upside potential. The price was right; the stars were properly aligned.

Thus it came to pass, after almost a year of twenty-five-dollar-a-month contributions and countless impassioned debates, that the Upper Granville Investment Club put its $2250 into slightly more than 25,000 shares of MUDEECO, Inc. This Los Alamos–based firm had manufactured a device that made it possible for apartment and condo owners to monitor and bill energy costs to the appropriate user, hence the full name: Multiple Unit Dwelling Energy Efficiency Corporation.

If this were Hollywood, rather than Central Vermont, MUDEECO would have skyrocketed in price, then split, then have been acquired, then went bust, with the ruralite investors hanging onto each twist and plummet of the roller coaster. Instead the stock immediately dropped thirty-five percent and stayed there. The investment club met religiously and reported on the nonactivity in great detail. After six such meetings, Darwin suggested they face the inevitable:

"This is as interesting as a slug race." He suggested they sell, take their losses, and invest the balance in a blowout dinner at Nino's Nook, Central Granville's best approximation of an eatery. The motion was passed unanimously.

The Central Vermont Boo-Ray League

Boo-Ray is a hybrid of bridge and poker that Darwin learned at his Dartmouth fraternity. The pots have an alarming tendency to grow quickly. After two delightfully entertaining evenings, a monster pot of three hundred dollars accumulated. Most of the pot was contributed by Townshend Clarke, whose total assets counted in seven digits but whose annual budget for entertainment was equal to Emil Dummerston Weed's monthly beer allowance.

To defuse the tension, Sammi suggested stopping the game and returning the money to the players. Everyone was agreeable except Townshend, who insisted that the game continue. On the next hand Tina Pisano won, but any exultation was short-circuited by Townshend and his wife, Sue the Shrew, launching into a bitter dispute, the gist of which was that Townshend was a complete fool for gambling away three hundred bucks when he was too cheap to take his wife out to an occasional dinner. The evening ended with Sue in tears, Townshend verbally disemboweled, and the rest of the attendees nervously gulping their drinks. Future Boo-Ray gatherings were discreetly cancelled in the interests of domestic tranquility.

The Gourmet Society

After a decade of potluck dinners, Darwin proposed a new, yuppified twist. Once per season the locals would gather at one couple's home, no kids allowed, for a repast of thematic culinary excellence. Hannah Duncan started the group off nicely with a sumptuous Scandinavian dinner, followed by the Pisanos' Palermo Pig-Out, which left community members grasping their girths and screaming for mercy. This idea was a winner, and the prospect of upcoming Gourmet Society gatherings became events of great anticipation.

Even the younger Blanchards, who normally eschewed any association with Flatlander frivolity, participated. Teresa, now successfully embarked upon a career as a salesperson for Mary Kay Cosmetics, welcomed the opportunity to broaden her culinary horizons. Bennett, while rarely touching the food served to him, found the pursuit harmless enough. Gourmet Society was toasted as the human bridge across the cultural abyss.

Then it came time for the Blanchards to host the society. For months prior, as per usual, speculation raged on what culinary delight awaited the group. Finally invitations were received for "Bennett's Banquet," a repast that turned out to be Bennett's favorite meal: scrambled eggs with ketchup, boiled potatoes, store-bought white bread, a big glass of milk, and the pièce de résistance, Betty Crocker Puddin' Cake.

Sue Clarke finally blurted out her displeasure. "The rest

of us," she said, "spent hours preparing for our meals. We polished the silverware and spent small fortunes on nice wines, and you serve us a meal bought at the IGA and gathered from the barn."

"It's my favorite food in the world," countered Bennett, clearly delighted at her displeasure, "and I wanted to share it with you."

The gulf between Chucks and Flatlanders widened, never again to be spanned by culinary means. "We are victims of our own pettiness," lamented Darwin, and while no one disagreed, the group could not figure a tactful way to meet without half the community getting bent out of shape.

The Community Hot Tub

The inspiration came to Darwin during the despair of Mud Season, when the world was nothing but a flaccid rut. Unable to do anything outside, and with the three kids creating mayhem within, he commandeered a baby-sitter and swept Sammi away for an evening of hedonism. They went north to Burlington, land of the legitimate yuppie (as opposed to the rural subspecies, of which the Hunters considered themselves members).

Even a nouveau Americaine meal, registering 4.2 on the Richter scale of pretension, did not eradicate the permeation of the mud. They tried a bottle of Piper Heidsieck champagne at forty-five bucks a pop, but still Darwin was not sated. He tried to explain his malaise to his wife:

"I mean, I really like the stuffed squash blossoms. And, don't get me wrong, mesquite-grilled shrimp with a raspberry-morel sauce is something you don't get in Upper

Granville every day. The salad was nice, even if I did have to pick all that cilantro shit off of everything. I'm not complaining. I just haven't gotten what I want out of the evening yet."

"And what do you want?" asked Sammi.

"I want warm. I want tropical. I want the feeling of Nairobi just after a summer shower. I want to steam clean my every pore, and to be so far away from cold, wet, and mud that I start thinking kindly of Vermont again."

Their waitron, Aaron, suggested a trip down the street to the Big Splash Hot Tub company. Aaron thereby earned a large tip and the dubious distinction of inspiring the creation of the Upper Granville Tubbies. Darwin and Sammi followed his advice, and after an hour of wallowing helplessly amid the steaming bubbles, Darwin whimpered that his wish had been granted.

The idea to form a community hot tub was spawned on the ride back. The very next night the neighborhood was summoned to the Hunters' for an organizational meeting. Response ranged from outrage (Walt Gunion) to exuberance (Hannah Duncan). Officers were named, assignments handed out, and goals set.

Twelve months and numerous meetings later, the group formally disbanded, not with a whimper, but with an appropriate big splash.

The group had always divided roughly into two factions, the compulsive organizers and the go-with-the-flow-ers. The former contingent established subcommittees on site selection, finance, maintenance, and equipment. They even generated a twenty-page set of bylaws that covered every contingency from death to failure to perform assigned maintenance.

The meetings of the Upper Granville Tubbies became lively social events, laced equally with starched decorum and a smirky bawdiness. After a year the group was ready to rock and roll. The rules were set, the equipment selected, the site known, and the dues paid. As a final disaster check, Darwin suggested that the group make a field trip to the Big Splash Hot Tubs.

The sense of anticipation was heightened by the feeling of doing something forbidden. Everyone tried to act nonchalant as they entered the Tidal Wave Room, with the Big Splash's twelve-man tub. No one made any rude comments about anyone's nipples or penises, not even Darwin, and for all the spirited buildup, the actual tubbing was enjoyably sedate.

The fireworks came one week later when the *Burlington Free Press* carried a page-one story reporting that a pornographic movie house in Montreal had been showing clips taken by a hidden camera at the Big Splash. Channel 3 showed the arraignment of the spa owners on the eleven o'clock news. They covered faces with jackets and looked very much the part of sin peddlers.

Sue the Shrew Clarke took the news particularly hard. Although there was no evidence that the Upper Granville contingent had made it onto the big screen in Montreal, she said she felt "violated," and sought the assistance of a rape crisis center in Montpelier. She blamed Darwin for her involvement in the whole sordid mess. He, in turn, fanned her wrath by reporting that Frenchmen from Quebec City to Thetford Mines were streaming to the X-rated theater in hopes of glimpsing "la bush de la belle Shrew."

Sue responded with a raised middle finger and a muttered obscenity. Townshend and Sammi clucked helplessly on the sidelines. Darwin took the incident one step too far when he hired a Quebeçois actor named Henri Thibodoux to show up in town one Saturday morning. Before people even had their coffee, there was Henri at the door, showing a tattered portrait of Sue and asking in fractured Franglaise where he might find the goddess.

"Not funny," said Sammi, staring coldly across the breakfast table.

"It better be," answered Darwin. "Cost me two hundred bucks. Besides, I've got nothing to lose. She hates my guts anyway, and I've never known why."

No one mentioned hot tubs much after that. While the Upper Granville Tubbies were not Darwin's last attempt to galvanize the community into concerted action, it represented a high-water mark. As the 1980s became more assertive, the people of Upper Granville, young and old, Flatlander and Chuck, slid into parallel paths of nuclear narcissism. First came the frenzy of childbearing, which doubled the valley population within six years. Next was the fitness movement, as the local residents strove to exorcise inexorable, impending middle age. And finally, the greatest threat of all to the community, the Age of Acquisition.

The Age of Acquisition began on January 23, 1983, when Walt and Martha Gunion bought an RCA VHS VCR for $1400. Until that time it was more fashionable not to own things. Townshend Clarke, for example, whose poverty-by-choice ethic was underlined by the monthly statements he received from Merrill Lynch, wore his home's lack of electricity and running water as proud badges.

Every month Walt procured a movie (this was before Central Granville had more video stores than churches) and invited everyone to watch it on his wide-screen Sony.

It was a miracle, everyone agreed. As prices lowered, others bought VCR's, and tape swapping became a neighborhood mania, limited only by Chuck/Flatlander aesthetic differences (Chuck Norris for Diane Keaton did not an equal trade make).

Joe Pisano caused a near revolt when he had the temerity to follow the advice of *Consumer Reports* and to cast his lot with video-disk technology. Two years later, when video disks had gone the way of lava lamps, and Joe had taken his player to the dump, Sammi Berger-Hunter still referred to him as a traitor.

Never again would a neighborhood member dare to break technological ranks. As they marched through materialistic life, be it computers (first Radio Shack, then Macintosh), compact-disk players (Fisher), lawn tractors (John Deere), and food processors (Cuisinart), they marched as one, a platoon of true patriots consuming the American way.

Then, in 1986, the Winkles moved into the Cowdrey House. They lasted less than six months, a tiny footnote in community history, but for the fact that they were the first to purchase a Plymouth Voyager. Hitherto, residents of the high valley had avoided expressing community identification via vehicular means. Darwin had his silver Saab Turbo, Townshend his perennial 1967 Volvo, Joe Pisano his panel van, Emil Dummerston Weed his International pickup. If people owned second cars, they tended to be faceless Japanese station wagons ("Itchipussies," Bennett Blanchard called them) riddled with body rot.

Then came the Winkles and a new era. Not only was their Voyager practical (room for kids, front-wheel drive), but luxurious. The Pisanos bought one with a sun roof; the Hunters countered with a sun roof and automatic shift.

Then Sue pried twenty grand from Townshend's trust fund and bought the tangerine flake, steamlined baby with fake wood paneling, power everything, and graphic equalizer. For two years there was a veritable plague of Voyagers, each more grand than the last. Comparisons of tomato varieties, recent movies, and woodstove efficiencies were replaced by debating the merits of cruise control, factory-installed roof racks versus component systems, and whether or not the custom luxury package paid for itself at trade-in time.

Even the Blanchards, both generations, bought Voyagers. "If someone told me that I'da paid seventeen thousand dollars for a car," mused Hoyt, "I'da thought he bin workin' in the barn too long."

For the Fourth of July parade the valley factions united, driving in formation like the tanks in Red Square on May Day. People called Upper Granville Voyagerville. Others called it the Yurpie Valley. Some invoked the words of Alton Blanchard, and called it simply Yonder.

It was just such historical developments that passed through the mind of Darwin Hunter in the days following Sammi's kick-butt campaign. He was reliving the past, contemplating the future, discussing it all with General Beauregard, mastering the possibilities. Soon, he said, I will launch into action. And when Darwin launches—

"Hey, King Kick Butt!" Darwin's mental proclamation was interrupted by a voice from the screen door. It was just past ten at night. Sammi and the kids were asleep, as was most of the Northland. Darwin recognized the voice as another denizen of the night, Gimp Fenvessey. He stood on the porch, holding the two plastic, gallon jugs that he filled daily from the Hunters' tap. Darwin invited him in with a laugh.

"Haven't they struck pay dirt yet? How far are they down?"

"A hundred and seventy-five feet. Walt's going berserk. He calls the well 'the money pit.' "

"Want a beer?" Darwin was glad for the prospect of late-night company more responsive than his dog.

"Always. Plus a shower. I need to get up to Montpelier first thing in the morning. Do you mind?"

Darwin shook his head amiably. He and Gimp were kindred souls in the Northern night. Despite a decade difference in age, they shared an intellectual curiosity and jaundiced outlook that made their conversations, invariably over a beer, lively and stimulating.

"What's happening in Montpelier?"

"The governor is giving a press conference. The regular bullshit."

"I've been thinking a lot about the regular bullshit, like what I'm going to do with the rest of my life."

"Jeezum, Darwin, don't get heavy on me. Are you serious about running for the State Senate?"

"Do you think I'm crazy?"

"Give me my beer before I answer." Darwin handed him a can of Miller Lite. Gimp opened it deftly with one hand. His deformed left arm—a "flipper," he called it— was the result of thalidomide. Gimp portrayed no sense of infirmity, using his quick wit and self-effacing humor instead to exude confidence bordering on cocksure. Although seemingly content to be a reporter for the *Clarion*, Gimp was also a stringer for several national publications, and his material—especially in regards to politics—was widely read and respected. Darwin kidded him about winning a Pulitzer prize one day, but Gimp knew that only the smallness of his stage prevented it.

He took a seat at the kitchen table. "Let me think. How would I assess your chances of beating Linwood 'Woody' Dunwoody in the race for the State Senate seat from the Fifth District? I would put the chances as roughly equivalent to winning the Tri-State Megabucks three weeks in a row, or of Bennett Blanchard leaving the farm to become a principal dancer in the New York City Ballet, or of my knocking out Mike Tyson in the first round. Let me express it a different way—"

"I get the point. You think I'm crazy."

"I didn't say that. I only said that your chances of winning are remote. Your decision to run should be based on your desire to participate in government, not your chances of winning."

"So you think it's okay to run, even if I don't have a snowball's chance in hell."

"Yes, I do, Darwin. As long as you are not mocking the system or playing games with it, or manipulating it for selfish reasons, I think you should run."

"That makes me feel a little better." There was a moment of silence. "I hate to admit my ignorance, but could you tell me a little bit about it?"

"About what?"

"About the government. About the state of Vermont. About Dunwoody. About everything. I am such a babe in the woods. I have no idea how anything works, let alone how to run a campaign. For some reason I'm compelled to take this wild idea that jumped out of my mouth on Riley Gore's show and to turn it into reality."

Gimp sipped on his beer, belched, then sipped again.

"Why don't you hang around with me a little, Darwin. Come up to the governor's press conference. I'll show you around the chambers. You don't have to rush into this thing. Even if you are going to run, you don't need to announce until the spring. Take your time. You don't want to make a mistake."

The next day Darwin learned that the government of the state of Vermont is divided into two governing chambers, a House of Representatives and a Senate. Each Senate district, a geographic entity synonymous with county, elects two representatives every other year. In total there are thirty-three state senators (Chittenden and Windsor counties get extra because of their concentrated population base), compared to one hundred fifty representatives. To be listed on the state ballot, a senatorial candidate must produce petitions by July eighteenth containing a minimum of one hundred signatures of district residents who do not object to seeing his name on the ballot. The primaries come the second Tuesday in September.

"By the way," asked Gimp, "which party are you?"

"I'ma party alla time," answered Darwin.

"I thought so," said Gimp. "Who did you vote for in the last election?"

"Refresh my memory, who ran?"

"You really are a novice in this, aren't you?"

"Is there a Dink Party? I've never been big on categorization."

"Establishing a party affiliation is simply a matter of logistical common sense. Your chances of being elected as a Republican or Democrat are infinitely greater than as an independent."

As a member of the Senate Darwin would be paid eighty-five-hundred dollars per annum for a legislative session that runs from January to May, four days a week. Being a state senator and holding down a full-time job is close to impossible unless one is self-employed, or has a sympathetic employer who can live with a worker who spends more time jawboning in Montpelier than anything else.

Darwin learned that Woody Dunwoody, a Republican, was a five-time incumbent with roots deeper in the Vermont soil than any maple tree. The son of an alcoholic logger, Dunwoody and his six brothers were a hard-drinking, hard-living lot whose initial claim to fame came in high school, when they brought Granville the only three state basketball championship flags the town had ever won.

Once they passed through their hell-raising stage, the Dunwoodys cornered strategic outposts in the greater Granville economic community. They counted among them a realtor, a tavern owner, an accountant, a banker, owner of the local building-supply outlet, a farmer, and a lawyer who was also a member of the State Senate. Collectively, they had the bases of Central Vermont well covered.

"What's he like?" Darwin asked Gimp on the ride back to Upper Granville.

"Personable," answered Gimp, lighting a cigarette with his good hand while steering with his flipper. "Salty, shrewd, devious, greedy, charismatic. Want some more adjectives?"

"No. What about this Natalie Weinstein?"

"She's the perfect opponent to Dunwoody, completely at the opposite end of the spectrum—if she runs, that is. She's just been through a fairly traumatic divorce, and even though she's raising quite a stir down at the law school, there are some who question whether or not she'll make a run for it.

"Natalie Weinstein is brilliant, ambitious, and has both a great killer instinct and the best legs around. She propped up that inane attorney general we had for five years, winning the respect of everyone in state government. She's intelligent, organized, and yet compassionate to the needs of the downtrodden."

"You mean like blacks and Hispanics," asked Darwin.

Gimp started laughing. "No, women—"

"And Flatlanders."

"And Quebecois."

"And dyslexics. How will she do in the election?"

"The dyslexics, the Quebecois, the homosexuals, the women, and Flatlanders will vote for her. Altogether she'll get forty-two percent of the vote, and it will be another landslide for Dunwoody. Let's be honest, a Jewish woman Flatlander has three strikes against her." Fenvessey's voice had such a note of finality that he was surprised when Darwin had a comeback.

"That's why Madeleine Kunin is governor of Vermont."

"Oh, yeah. I forgot."

"How will my presence in the race effect things?"

"The same way my paycheck affects the Consumer Price Index—not at all." Gimp saw this comment was devastating to his friend. "Hey, don't let it get you down. I already told you that you can't win. The world needs candidates like you to keep things in perspective. Besides, if you do win, there are great fringe benefits."

"Like what?"

"Well, like your very own cluttered desk in the Senate chamber, and a portion of a file-cabinet drawer. Plus, you get to use the communal Xerox machine. You get bathroom privileges, but no shower, only the Speaker of the House gets a shower, but that doesn't matter, because you can always shower at the sleazy motels that cater to the politicos. Then there is the privilege of waiting in the lunch line to spend four-fifty for a plate of overdone pork, plus a cup of Vermont milk, God forbid you drink anything else.

"But it doesn't stop here. There's a communal WATS line that enables you to have conversations with demanding constituents or groveling lobbyists in complete privacy from the rest of the world. Have I left out anything? Of course, free parking! You have a daily opportunity to play bumper cars with what is universally regarded as the most inadequate parking lot north of Yankee Stadium. What more could a man want?"

"I have only one thing to say," said Darwin, staring out the window at the rapidly coloring foliage. "Let's stop for some beer."

Darwin deemed phase one of his campaign "The Big Picture." Before formally announcing his candidacy, he would listen to his constituency, spend time talking to people, hear their concerns, understand this point in regional history. How might he best lead?

Toward this end he spent his spare time in the next few weeks going door to door, not just in Upper Granville, but in the greater metropolis of Center Granville (population 4800). What he found surprised him.

Everyone had heard of his pledge, uttered in the privacy of his own home to his own wife, to kick butt.

So you're the Butt Kicker! We saw you on TV. Is Riley Gore as genuine off camera as he is on? We're glad to see you run. Vermont needs some butt kicked.

Unfortunately, no one could agree whose butt needed kicking. Some wanted him to kick Linwood "Woody"

Dunwoody's butt for being in office so long. Some wanted Natalie Weinstein's butt kicked for being a woman. Others wanted her butt kicked for being Jewish, or a Flatlander, or a lawyer. Some wanted police chief Mulcady's butt kicked for taking a leave of absence to enter a substance-abuse clinic. Other nominations for posterior thrashing were Liam Cameron, the leader of the Community Players theater group, who absconded after a performance of *Camelot* with all funds and the Presbyterian minister's wife. Or Malcolm Kidder, the bank president, now facing charges involving a sex-for-pay ring of adolescent boys in Burlington. Or Jana Addison, director of the community preschool, facing abuse charges brought by her own husband.

Others expressed preference for group butt kicking. Kick the school board's tight-assed butt, and while you're at it, the road crew's, which never gets here until the selectman's driveway is plowed. And kick snow mobilers' butts because they make too much noise, and the same goes for the teenagers who hang out by the video machine down to the Quik-Stop. When you're done, kick the butts of those religious groups who are holier than thou, and the butts of all do-gooders too. Don't forget the fat butts of fat cats.

Some stated bluntly that Darwin should be the kickee rather than the kicker. When Darwin pointed out the physical impossibility of kicking oneself, they often suggested an equally impossible alternative.

After several weeks his market research was complete. "I now have the big picture," said Darwin to General Beauregard, dozing peacefully in his study. "People are pissed off. It doesn't matter that Dunwoody and his brothers are providing loans, credit, and jobs. It doesn't matter that Weinstein has an IQ of a hundred sixty. People are frustrated by an erosion of morals on the part of their supposed leaders. They've been lied to too many times. It's happening here, it's happening in Washington, it's happening at the Kremlin, it's happening on the nightly news. They're confused and defeated. They're giving up!"

Indeed, the concerns of the community were shared on a broader scale. Headlines were filled with tales of religious leaders bilking their flocks while shacking up with bimbos. Political candidates lied and plagiarized while they, too, romped with the bimbos. Government employees were revealed to be zealots whose patriotism was irrevocably entwined with elaborate scams of bribery and deception.

Darwin's research created a portrait of a world not unlike a waterlogged baseball: its shape was intact, but its seams were stretched and rotting from within.

"Holy mackerel!!" he exclaimed, working himself into a frenzy that General Beauregard placidly observed. "This shit's gotta stop." He was beginning to glimpse the big picture, and both the size and condition of the canvas overwhelmed him. "Give the people a truly honest man and they will follow him to the moon. Everyone is losing confidence, because they have been lied to so often by the people they trust. They're sick of it! And they want to kick butt, or they want me to kick butt, or they want to kick my butt. They're not sure what they want. But more than ever, they need someone they can trust."

The General looked up at him from the worn, braided throw rug on the wide pine floor of Darwin's study. His expression spoke to Darwin as if the dog could enunciate as clearly as Sir John Gielgud.

"Get real, Master. No one cares about honesty or trust.

All people want is someone who will tell them what they want to hear and who will remember their names once a year."

"Oh yeah? Well you're just as jaded as everyone else. You sound like you're from goddamn Short Hairs, New Jersey. But you're missing the point, my furry friend. You're missing the point of what Vermont is all about. Up here you can make a difference. Up here democracy works! That's why I want to be King, or whatever it is I'm running for."

"Then you should run," the General said.

"Sure," said Darwin, "that's easy for you to say, but I'm not what you'd call a moral paragon. There is lots of stuff I've done that I'm not exactly proud of."

No one asked you to be perfect, the General countered, only to be honest. There's a difference, you know.

"I know," responded Darwin, lapsing into repetition so that his mind could grasp a dramatic concept, "I know, I know, I know, I know." With each repetition his conviction grew.

3

Bumps

To compare Hannah Duncan to B. J. Bosco, her prede-
cessor in the Upper Granville schoolhouse, was unfair,
misleading, and inevitable. Both were single women. Both
were strong and independent. Here the similarities ended
and the opposites began. Hannah was thin and hard, a
gray piece of slate with a face etched upon it. B.J. was
round, blond, and slothful, but witty and irreverent. She
could guzzle beer with Emil, then whip him in arm wres-
tling. She overwhelmed the Walt Gunions of the world by
spinning them around. Hannah accomplished the same
thing with an unwavering stare.

At the age of sixty-one Hannah ran five miles a day,
consistently winning her category in local road races. She
loved beating men, and humiliated Darwin in her first
Running of the Valley (an annual run around the Upper
Granville Valley) by finishing with a kick that left the
younger man making excuses for the coming year.

Because Hannah had successfully challenged the Darwins of the world, she had become a spiritual guru for the

Flatlander women of the valley. After all, didn't Hannah lead a man-free life, discarding or outliving three husbands? Didn't she live alone in the rural north, defying the elements with three cats and a four-wheel-drive Subaru? Didn't she manage both a career (hospital administrator) and motherhood (a grown daughter, living in Denver)?

On the Chuck side, Teresa Blanchard was comfortable with the fact that she had softened in the middle after four children. The farm was always cash poor, so selling Mary Kay Cosmetics provided a natural and much needed outlet for both her creativity and aggressiveness. She was also active politically, spearheading the Farm Wives Against E.R.A. movement that lobbied successfully against the passage of the bill, much to the chagrin of the Sue Clarkes and Sammi Berger-Hunters.

Across the cultural valley, the women experienced the same metamorphosis as Teresa, but with radically different plumage:

Tina Pisano—sweet, meek, timid Tina, daughter of an Italian and wife to an Italian—had the temerity to strap on running shoes and discover she was fleet as a doe. She became as addicted to running and aerobics as she was devoted to her family.

Sue found success, or rather, it found her. It started when Townshend traded an antique cook stove for a pair of Nubian goats. The goats produced more milk than they could drink, so Sue experimented with making goat-milk yogurt. The finished product was superb, balancing perfectly a bacterial tartness with the texture and wholesomeness of the udder.

Sue packaged small amounts for sale at the Onion River Food Coop. A jar found its way into the hands of "Slinging

Stevie" Mugford, the sharpshooting guard who joined the Boston Celtics in the twilight of his career.

Once an all-star, Mugford was now reduced to cameo appearances during garbage time at the end of blow-outs. Red Auerbach, the shrewd general manager of the Celtics, maintained him principally to provide a stabilizing influence on the young bucks on the team. In a time of post-adolescent millionaires self-destructing via cocaine, Slinging Stevie was known for obsessive clean-living. Upon arriving in Boston, his first act was to procure a source of goat milk, a search that led eventually to the Onion River Food Coop and an introduction to Sue Clarke's unique yogurt.

No one paid much attention to Slinging Stevie, let alone his passion for goat-milk yogurt, until the first game of the playoffs against the Atlanta Hawks, when the journeyman came off the bench after two of the regular guards were ejected in a brawl. Mugford hit eleven consecutive shots, leading a miraculous Celtic comeback. After the game the hero attributed his performance to the goat-milk yogurt that came from a farm somewhere in the middle of Vermont. Since the final hoop had been shot right over the outstretched arms of Atlanta's Dominique Wilkins, a sportswriter coined the name "In Yo' Face Yogurt," and a business was born.

Slinging Stevie continued his post-season dream, leading the Celtics to victory after victory, and ultimately the championship. It was the sports story of the eighties, and Sue's In Yo' Face Vermont Yogurt played a prominent role. Demand skyrocketed, and Sue found herself atop a business growing as fast as Tomar Brook, the valley watershed, during the spring thaw.

Sammi Berger-Hunter's reentry was on a different path.

Always active politically, she maintained official positions in Mothers Against Drunk Driving, Vermont Chapter of the National Organization of Women, Women's Anti-Nuclear Coalition, and other groups that Darwin lumped together as "ladies' clubs." Increasingly she spent spare time auditing courses at the Vermont Law School, and Darwin suspected that within the year she would announce her intention to enroll.

The Flatlander women referred to each other as "neat ladies," and met frequently to network and nurture. Teresa Blanchard, whose unpopular stance on the Equal Rights Amendment branded her as a traitor to the sex, was a notable omission.

On Halloween, Darwin and Joe Pisano talked Bennett Blanchard into giving up thirty pumpkins that were destined for the compost heap anyway. It was a violation of Bennett's nature to give away anything for free. The two men, aided by their respective eldest sons, Bobby (Pisano, age eleven) and Duke (Hunter, age nine), scooped and carved for the better part of an afternoon. As darkness descended, they built a bonfire with a kettle of mulled cider contributed by Hoyt Blanchard. By the time the kids arrived, a ragtag collection of Strawberry Shortcakes and Masters of the Universe, the air was atingle with moonlight, spiced apples, and candle-scorched pumpkins. The kids ran as a tribal pack from home to home, always within sight of the bonfire and the moon, while the adults prodded embers and chuckled in their self-satisfaction. Later, as kids gorged on candy, the elders adjourned to the Hunters' kitchen, where they guzzled their own confections, beer and wine.

Emil Dummerston Weed, a quintessential practitioner

of the woodchuck lifestyle, became extremely loquacious and amusing after the third beer. Darwin always made sure to serve him three right away. Emil took special pleasure in telling stories or doing things to offend the women from the Flatlands. Most of his pranks were harmless—such as when he offered a bucket of steaming cow innards from a just-slaughtered beast to Martha Gunion—but occasionally they crossed the boundary of good taste. Whenever he made such a foray, Darwin was usually right there with him.

This night Emil decided to hold court on the subject of incest. The Weeds of Granville are a farflung clan, many of whom still dwell on the fringes of civilization and all of whom sport the wild blue eyes and yellow teeth to give credence to even the wildest rumors.

Emil shocked the crowd with the statement that he was unsure of his own parentage. He interwove a lineage of brothers marrying sisters, and mothers taking up with sons, that held everyone sickeningly spellbound until he pushed the limits of credibility too far by saying he had fathered a child by his own mother.

"You're disgusting," snapped Tina Pisano.

"And this is not a subject to joke about," added Hannah Duncan. "It still goes on."

Emil laughed his hyena laugh. "I'm telling God's honest truth," he protested between gulps. "I tell you I am, or my name ain't Uncle Dad."

"I was once almost arrested for incest," said Joe Pisano. Since Joe tended toward soft-spoken seriousness, as opposed to the Emils and Darwins of the world, his statement brought instant silence to the crowd.

"Honey, don't tell this story," pleaded Tina.

"It's all right," he replied, touching her arm and looking her directly in the eye. "We're among friends.

"It was just before we moved to Vermont. We lived in a three-room apartment in Somerville. We were invited to this big Italian wedding, so we got my twelve-year-old niece to babysit. We expected to be back late, so we told my niece to just go to bed in our bedroom when she got tired. We would sleep on the fold-out couch in the living room.

"It was a typical Italian wedding. By the end we had drunk so much guinea red that we couldn't see straight. We got home, flopped into bed, and went to sleep. Everything would have been fine, except sometime during the night I had to get up and pee. I'm still groggy as hell, and so, out of habit, I turn right from the bathroom toward our bedroom, forgetting that I'm supposed to be on the Hide-A-Bed.

"I flop into bed, oblivious to everything, and am asleep in two seconds. My niece, meanwhile, is lying there petrified. She stares at the ceiling, rigid as a board, then gets out of bed, tiptoes through the apartment, and walks back to my brother's house.

"They've been to the same wedding and are equally out of it. My brother, who's more Italian than I am, if you can believe it, hears this garbled story about me climbing into bed with his daughter and goes charging out of the house, swearing to kill me. His wife, knowing that her husband is A, still drunk, and B, Italian, calls the cops.

"My brother and the cops arrive at the same time. They walk right in the house, and I wake up from my peaceful sleep with flashlights in my face and my brother threatening to kill me."

Joe's story produced rapt attention and a few uneasy smiles and snickers. For the most part no one knew quite how to react. Finally, Sammi spoke:

"Joe, is this a true story?"

Joe looked at her with his sincere brown eyes, and replied: "It's the God's honest truth, or my name ain't Uncle Dad."

Joe's and Emil's stories reminded some of the unfortunate Norry Barnham incident. Norry Barnham was a smiling, plump girl of fourteen who lived with six brothers and sister and a widowed father in a doublewide on a remote road midway between Upper Granville and Center Granville. Norry, short for "Eleanor," had been the subject of much talk among the Flatlander women. Granted, she was clearly of Chuck lineage, but in her flowering adolescence there existed the potential creation of a new generation of female alliance. We must, the ladies had clucked over Amaretto-flavored decaffeinated (water-extraction method) coffee, freshly brewed with gobs of whipped cream, find a way to help Norry achieve her full potential.

Norry began babysitting at age eleven, her experience with younger siblings giving her maturity well beyond her years. Moreover, her effervescent disposition and willingness to accommodate even the most frantic last-minute requests had made her a key component in the emancipation of the valley women.

"She's so bright," sighed Sammi. "And pretty," added Tina. "How can we save her from becoming another Teresa Blanchard?" said Sue.

The community fixation on Norry had increased with the passage of time and the obvious flowering of her own womanhood. "Uh-oh," said Darwin one summer day when Norry arrived wearing an elasticized halter top, "bumps. Once the local tomcats see those, this babysitter will be history."

Indeed, the prospect of the community protégé being slobbered upon by the youthful Emil Dummerston Weeds of Central Vermont had filled the Flatlander mothers with revulsion. Was Norry doomed to spend a life as had her mother, married to a half-wit who kept her oppressed, knocked up, and ignorant? Not if they could help it.

One night the Pisanos had returned from an evening of foreign film and Mexican food. Joe took Norry home. Tina avoided, as did her valley peers, contact with the Barnham home. No one had actually met Euclid "Butcher" Barnham. He was a mountain man who drove a logging truck with a sign on the door: THE LONG LOST LOGGER. He had a wild black and gray beard, three fingers on his left hand, and teeth that had never encountered fluoride. From the disheveled appearance of the yard and the man, it was assumed that the inside of the Barnham house would befit a Stephen King novel.

On this night Norry was babbling to Joe a nonstop, teenage account of the trivial events of the evening. Her mood darkened as they turned onto the steep drive that led to her home.

"Oh, Daddy's gonna be mad," she moaned, " 'cuz I didn't clean up the kitchen before I left. I promised I would, then Mrs. Pisano called and I forgot. He'll probably make me kiss his wienie."

By this time the car had reached a halt in front of the Barnham doublewide. Norry opened the door and bounded out as lightly as ever, but not before a summary statement to Joe: "And he's been making me kiss his wienie a lot lately. My little brother Chad too. Oh well . . . 'night,

Mr. Pisano." She rolled her eyes, then turned to go.

Joe always waited a few seconds to make sure she was safely inside before leaving. This time he waited even longer, numbed by the expectation of screams and gunshots. Instants before, Norry had been a carefree, babbling teenager. Now, in Joe's mind, she had been sent to a squalid, Appalachian doom, forced to submit to the most exploitive of villains, her own kin, so naïve and trusting that she would mention her humiliation to a complete stranger.

It occurred to Joe that the confession was a plea for help. Should he go inside? He remained in the car, paralyzed. He left only when a three-fingered hand pulled aside the living-room curtain.

The next morning Joe related the story to Tina. Her reaction was swift—she convened Sammi and Sue for a council meeting. Their conclusion was unanimous—they had to involve Hannah. For a week they discussed alternatives. Advice from Darwin that they mind their own business was summarily dismissed.

Kidnapping was considered. Eventually, fact finding was settled upon as the most legitimate course of action. Norry was called by Sammi and hired for a Friday evening of babysitting. When she arrived, however, she encountered a solo Hannah Duncan, armed with a small cassette recorder. Hannah sympathetically and discreetly probed her on the horrendous father and the insatiable wienie.

Hannah emerged with a bleary-eyed Norry after a half-hour. She sent the girl to watch television with the Hunter children while the adults in the kitchen learned of their mistake.

"The dread 'wienie,' " said a downcast Hannah, "is her

father's pinkie finger, on which he wears a silver ring that belonged to his dead wife. Whenever the kids need inspiration, they get it from the memory of their mother."

It was anticlimactic when Butcher Barnham wheeled the Long Lost Logger into the village of Upper Granville mere minutes after Norry returned home from the conversation with Hannah. Darwin answered the door, finding himself face to face with epic rage.

"Who's responsible?" boomed the Butcher, his thunderous voice scattering the Hunter children to the sanctity of their bedrooms.

A reedy voice came from behind Barnham. Hannah Duncan had heard the rumble of the truck and come right over.

"I am." There was not even the slightest quaver of fear.

"That's the one, Daddy," said Norry weakly. Her father turned to face Hannah.

"You bring my daughter to babysit. Upset her by nosing into our family life. Tape-record it! I don't know what's going on with you people in this valley. I've heard wild stories, but I've chose to mind my own business. I should be screaming about authorities and jail, but I'm just saying one thing, that none of my children are allowed down here again. I promise you that."

The father and daughter walked as one to the logging truck. He helped her climb in through the driver's side, then he followed. The Long Lost Logger could be heard rumbling down the road for a very long time after it was out of sight. He left a lot of silence in his wake. And the silence remained until Townshend Clarke opened his big mouth and reminded everyone how the road to humility can be lined by the most noble intentions.

* * *

The next morning Darwin was, as usual, the first Sunday-morning customer at the Granville General Store. (Sometimes he arrived even before the newspaper delivery vans for the *Burlington Free Press* and *Rutland Times Herald*). On this bleak Sunday the air was bereft of color or moisture. His Saab raised a dusty fishtail as he streaked down the access road. Inside, the store was warm and woody. Fresh coffee was on the warmer. Behind the counter Howard "Warren" Pease was reading the *New York Times*.

"Good morning, Senator. How goes the campaign?" said Warren.

Darwin came one step inside the store and wavered, a hand clutched to his brow and his shoulders swaying from side to side as if an earthquake moved beneath him.

"I . . . don't . . . feel . . . well," he stammered.

Warren had enough experience with Darwin not to look up from the paper. "A tough Halloween, Darwin?"

"I think . . . I'm seeing . . . a . . . a . . . *New York Times* in the Granville General Store."

"That's right. Want me to start reserving you one?"

"Oakley would turn in his grave." Darwin invoked the name with reverence. Oakley McBean had resisted any change in the store that might have been construed as a concession to Flatlander interests.

"Had to," said Warren simply. "I did a little analysis." He then went on to explain the program he had set up on his Macintosh, using the Lotus 1–2–3 spreadsheet to create a series of what ifs to show that carrying the *New York Times* would, in the course of his lifetime, add some $82,364 in gross revenues to his business, netting a profit of $21,005. Provided, of course, that the assumptions of the actuarial tables were accurate.

"These figures," he added gratuitously, "do not factor in the value of capital."

"Spare me. You still carry the local papers, I assume. Where's the *Free Press*?"

"Right over there behind the condom display."

Darwin stared at him for a full measure. "Do we really need a condom display in the Granville General Store?"

Warren was matter-of-fact: "I give my customers what they want. If they want the *New York Times*, I give them the *Times*. If they want Jogbras, I carry Jogbras."

"You carry Jogbras?"

"And they're selling very well, thank you. More women run in this valley than darn socks. Hannah Duncan told me they would sell, and they have."

"What about the condoms? Stella Blanchard must get a kick out of those. Hey, some of these look pretty exotic."

"Oh sure, interesting thing about the condom business . . ." Anytime Warren began a sentence with "interesting thing," it prefaced a lengthy cruise into a sea of tedium. In the case of condoms, Warren presented a fact-filled monologue on how the publicity surrounding the AIDS epidemic had attracted an excess of venture capital to the industry. As a result the industry now produced enough condoms for each man in the world to have sex twice an hour. The excess competition, in turn, created a scramble to define market niches by way of product differentiation.

"Look at these things," said Warren, spinning the rack. "We got every flavor, color, and size you can imagine. We got 'em with gewgaws and ticklies and zebra stripes and little love nubs."

"Listen to this," said an incredulous Darwin, as he read from one of the brightly colored boxes. " 'Love nubs will

do for your lovemaking what wine does for your appetite.'
Who buys these things?"

"You wouldn't believe it, Darwin—women. In fact,
most of the women in the valley have bought some of
these. Hannah Duncan told me they'd be moneymakers,
and she was right. Sue's bought some, Hannah, of course,
Sammi, and Tina. Just about everyone."

Warren rattled on, telling Darwin about the return per
square foot that condoms produced compared to other
products. Darwin appeared to listen, but was lost in
thought. It was not just that Warren was boring, but a
question glazed Darwin's visage: Why, three years after
his vasectomy, was his wife buying condoms?

4

The Transformation of Townshend

The signals for an explosion surrounded Townshend Clarke, but once it arrived, it caught even those closest to him by surprise. Despite an exterior as placid as Bennett Blanchard's best milker, his history was not of stability, but overreaction. As a teenager in Rhode Island, Townshend was caught up in the sixties revolution and expressed his outrage by "blowing up" the Mashpaug Country Club with a pathetic bomb made from tens of thousands of caps for toy pistols.

The attempted revolution failed, and Townshend's parents covered for him. Boys will be boys, don't you know? Heh-heh, nothing of interest for the readers of your newspaper here. Townshend joined the Army, went to Vietnam, came home, married, inherited a million bucks, chucked it all, and came to live as a pauper in Vermont. Life as a Chuck-by-choice went smoothly enough until the horizon of forty came into Townshend's ken. Here he was, living at the northern antipodes of Appalachia, earning less even than Emil Dummerston Weed, embracing a lifestyle that the rest of the world had left behind at the turn of the century. His sense of inadequacy was only heightened by Sue's success with In Yo' Face Yogurt.

It was a Saturday during the dead space between leaf season and real winter. Peepers from Metuchen to Cos Cob had had their annual gawk and were back in the Flatlands watching football games. Darwin Hunter, who described himself as a feral Flatlander, raked the few remaining leaves in a steady cold drizzle. It was a futile activity. Soon the blanket of snow would fall, and when it finally disappeared in spring, there would be just as many leaves as there were now. Mostly, the activity freed him from the din of ritual Saturday-morning cartoons.

Dink-dink-dink. A metallic tapping drew his eyes up to the eastern hillside banking the valley. The sound was soft enough to go unnoticed in most environments, but in a land of stimulus deprivation, where even the scratching of a leaf rake against the earth is an intrusion, it drew Darwin's immediate attention. He looked up to see Townshend Clarke tapping a steel rod into the earth with the blunt end of a splitting maul. His friend was dwarfed by the hillside. He looked up, caught Darwin's gaze, and waved.

An unexplained activity such as this was sure to inspire the ruralite's curiosity. Why would Townshend hammer a stake into the ground in the rain? His actions, despite the wave, had a furtive quality. Darwin noticed a fluorescent ribbon tied around the stake. A property marker? Now why, Darwin asked himself, would Townshend be putting up a property marker on a hillside that belonged to the Blanchard family?

Townshend walked down the hill to the road, and in a matter of seconds Walt Gunion's black Oldsmobile appeared and picked him up. They passed Darwin with a neighborly wave but no explanation. Darwin was curious, yet unconcerned. Mysteries in rural life do not last long. He would learn about it by and by.

The drizzle had turned into little slush pellets when the next incident occurred. Bennett Blanchard roared by on his John Deere, his visage contorted with rage and loathing. He ignored Darwin's howyadoin' and proceeded directly to the hillside from whence Townshend had come. He stormed up the hill, a Marine taking Iwo Jima, and wrestled the stake from the ground. He then carried it over to the edge of the woods, wound up like an Olympic hammer thrower and hurled it. Darwin did not bother waving to Bennett on the return trip. If Bennett was pissed off at Townshend, it would mean he was pissed off at all Flatlanders.

"What was that?" asked Sammi, attracted by Bennett's noisy wake.

"I'm not sure," answered Darwin, "but I feel we are about to witness yet another rural roar."

Sammi nodded; the phrase "rural roar" was a private joke they shared. Last July, just after dinner on a warm night, Darwin suggested going out for ice cream cones for dessert. Despite the reputation of Vermont as home to Ben and Jerry's gourmet ice cream in a thousand zany flavors, for most Vermonters a summer ice cream means a vanilla soft-serve on a cardboard cone. They call it "going for a Creemee," and although the experience pales alongside a Brigham's coffee sugar cone with chocolate jimmies on the Boston Common, it's still the best show in town.

The family piled into the Voyager and drove to Granville's premier drive-in, the CreeMee Queen. Unfortunately, the rest of Central Vermont had the same idea.

Darwin waited in line for more than twenty minutes, so was a touch testy when he brought the cones back to the picnic table where the family awaited him. The table beside them had a group of six Chucks who had spent the afternoon swilling beer in a battered Oldsmobile. They were now totally drunk, and less patient than Darwin's kids about the inefficiencies of the CreeMee Queen.

Just as the tongues of the Hunter clan touched their long-awaited cones, one of the Chucks produced a boom box that began punching out rap music at more than a hundred decibels. Darwin and Sammi, tongues on cone, exchanged glances. Her look said, "Aren't you going to do something?" and his, "Yeah, but I haven't figured out what." Sammi took matters into her own hands.

"You are too drunk to even consider driving. You're going to kill someone's child. I'm reporting you to the authorities."

Luckily the music was too loud for them to decipher her speech. One among them—the biggest, ugliest, and meanest—got up and pitched over to Darwin, sticking a stubbled face, a mask of belligerence, directly into his.

"Whashee say 'bout'r mooshic?"

Darwin noticed that the man had a variety of homemade tattoos. In fact, on his hairy knuckles was etched FUCK YOU! A second behemoth had now risen to join the fray. Darwin reached deep into his bag of tricks, developed from years of being what Sammi described as a dink. He shouted to be heard over the funky sound:

"She asked if you had any Beastie Boys tapes."

"I thawshee dint lik'da mooshic."

"Naw, can you turn it up? The kids want to dance when they finish their cones." The second guy, while even drunker than the first, turned out to be a peacemaker. He commandeered he of the Fuck You! fingers back to the picnic table, then came back to apologize.

"Sorry, Mac. My fren's feelin' a l'il too good. We'nt wanna shtart 'nother rur'l roar."

An interesting phrase, thought Darwin, "rural roar." Surprisingly literate, with complex overtones of meaning, and a certain onomatopoetic sound.

"No," he replied, accepting the proffered hand, "we don't want another rural roar either."

The man held on to his hand: "I served'n Vietnam. Lass thing I wanna do now's shtarta third rur'l roar."

Thenceforth, for Darwin and Sammi, any confrontation in the Northland, especially one with a predictable conclusion, became (yet another) rural roar.

The Saturday weather worsened from miserable to excruciating. The slush pellets became big and gooey and accumulated on all horizontal surfaces. This placed an unrealistic burden on the trees, whose branches still held vestigial leaves. The additional weight caused the limbs to fall, generally onto power lines, and by noon there was no power in Central Vermont.

After a lunch of bean soup warmed on the woodstove, Darwin convinced the kids to come outside and scrape together the first snowman of the season. It was pretty funky, as the snowballs were covered with leaves and dirt. By the time they finished "Grimy the Snowman," they were ready for an afternoon of checkers.

Life centered around the woodstove. Candles were gathered and water drawn off into pots for what could be a long journey into the past. Darwin regaled the children with stories of life in the good old days, not Upper Granville at the turn of the century, but Cincinnati, where he grew up in the 1950s. So he lied a little bit! The kids loved it.

Dinner was angel-hair pasta with marinara sauce. He and Sammi sipped on a robust Gamay Beaujolais that made the candlelight flicker and dance even more. Maybe it was an illusion, but Darwin felt that his bedtime story, about the time Max Headroom came to Upper Granville, was even more clever than usual.

The signs of Townshend's transformation had been apparent for a long time, but the pattern was clear only in retrospect. For more than ten years he lived in the ascetic stringency of a leaky farmhouse without power or any of the comforts of the twentieth century. He chose to ignore constant beratement from a wife who correctly referred to his inaccessible trust fund as a "lack-of-trust" fund. He still wore the same flannel shirt for weeks at a time, and when he changed, it was into an identical shirt. He wore one of the few ponytails left in Vermont, although his hairline had crept steadily northward. He drove only a 1967 Volvo, just like his parents', which he'd smashed up two decades earlier. Now he bought old Volvos two at a time, spending hours salvaging parts that might become useful at a later date.

The first big change occurred shortly after the Stowe Stallion left town. Townshend assumed the mantle of the protector of the town's architectural tradition, keeping Upper Granville free from trailers, satellite dishes, and aluminum siding. He read extensively on the subject, and even made crude attempts to mimic the Stallion's trademark haughtiness.

His wife's desire for a more normal home was granted, obsessively so. The Clarke home was restored and modernized in an agonizing process that lasted for more than three years, during which the family's standard of living actually went downhill. The original house was, in effect, taken to the dump, stick by stick. In its place rose an identical structure with every imaginable modern feature encased in a colonial shell that obsessively hid its contemporary innards. There was distinct illogic to the renovation. Why, for instance, build in an electronic security system and then put on colonial latches that do not lock? Even if the doors could be locked and the system thereby activated, the Granville police department was not equipped to acknowledge or respond to such a high-tech alarm.

Emil Dummerston Weed had the right idea for rural security, the bumper sticker on his pickup reading: THIS VEHICLE PROTECTED BY SMITH & WESSON.

The Clarke house also had a built-in vacuum system, electronic garage-door openers, room-to-room intercom, and even piped-in music to the barn so that Sue's goats could produce milk to the strains of Vivaldi. Moreover, the wide pine floors were buffed to a soft luster, the cabinetry was hand-finished raised-panel with beveled noses created by antique planes, and the wainscoting had original milk paint.

The progress of the house was community business. Typically, one began a conversation with an expression of sympathy for Sue and the children, who faced another winter of the Portosan toilet in the backyard as the restoration of the bathroom continued. The next comment would be to the effect that it sure would be beautiful when it was done. Then, for the rest of the hour, the participants would alternately marvel and rail on what a fool Townshend Clarke must be to spend hundreds of thousands to create a house that would ultimately be worth one third its investment. Ultimately, however, everyone conceded Townshend's innate right as a Vermonter to be as foolish as he pleased about his own house.

Darwin and Sammi sat silently in the candlelight, waiting for the power to return. The slush storm had abated; the woodstove provided warmth, but it could not thaw the coolness that separated them. They made small talk about the children, the storm. The phone mercifully rang. Darwin was closest.

"Hello?"

"Hey, B.K., ready to move south?" It was Townshend Clarke IV.

"B.K.?" asked Darwin, puzzled.

"Butt Kicker! So did you boot any bottoms today?"

"Nah, somedays you need a break from the same old routine." Darwin hoped that his voice would convey how bored he had become with this routine.

Townshend just marched forward. "Listen, buddy, why I called, I want to make an appointment with you. I'll need an hour and a half of undivided attention."

"What's up?"

"I can't tell you on the phone, but it's something exciting. How about Tuesday night, seven-thirty?"

"Okay with me. Want me to fire up the sauna?"

"No, I have some things to show you. And Walt will be with me. So, Tuesday night?"

Darwin took in a breath. This was weird. He confirmed the night and before saying good night mentioned to Townshend that Bennett Blanchard had thrown the metal stake into the woods. Townshend laughed:

"I expected that. Bennett's so . . . so . . . rigid. Know what I'm saying? Tuesday. 'Bye."

Darwin walked back to the kitchen. Sammi looked up and asked who was on the phone.

"Townshend," said Darwin thoughtfully, "but it wasn't like any Townshend I've ever talked to. He seemed so . . ." The word escaped Darwin for several seconds. Finally it came to him. ". . . confident." The juxtaposition of his friend's name and this word was as unlikely as snow on a green hillside.

"Poor Sue," sighed Sammi, not picking up Darwin's sense of something amiss. "She puts up with so much from that guy."

Darwin was late arriving home on Tuesday. There was a Lincoln Town Car, a hundred yards long, sitting in the Hunter driveway, a real pimpmobile with many gratuitous doodads. He walked into the kitchen, where Sammi was sitting with Walt Gunion and a completely bald man in a blue suit. Sammi's face wore an unmistakable expression of concern. Darwin's heart fluttered:

"Sammi! What's wrong?"

"Darwin." She spoke slowly, with great deliberation, and an understated sense of drama. "I'd like you to meet Townshend Clarke the Fourth."

If a picture is worth a thousand words, then a ten-second stare is worth a million. Darwin took it all in—the shaved head, the tiny diamond stud in the left earlobe, the thousand-dollar suit. Townshend even reeked of Giorgio cologne for men instead of his more familiar scent of sawdust, straw, and animals.

"I suppose that's your land yacht in the driveway?" Darwin asked dumbly. Townshend nodded. Darwin continued, "So, this is the official mid-life crisis."

"No," said Townshend, his voice authoritative and af-

71

firmative, even in the negative. "This is business. I just looked around at my life, and I've been at one point too long. Everyone else—Joe, you, Sue, Sammi, even Bennett—has grown, but I've been standing still, making the same statement over and over. I want to do something meaningful with my life, and it's just taken me a long time to figure out what that was going to be."

"And now you know?"

"And now I know."

"And that's what I'm going to find out about tonight?"

"That's right."

"It's not religion?" Darwin asked squeamishly.

"It's not religion."

"Okay. Let me get a beer. And let me get you and Walt a beer, and you can come in the other room and lay it on me. Why did you shave your head?"

"Darwin, it was getting a little thin on top. I knew I couldn't pull this off looking like a hippie, but when they cut off the ponytail, I looked like Walter Mitty. I'm going to be high profile in this thing, so I decided I might as well be memorable. You like it?"

"I hate it, and you smell funny."

"Let's go in the other room."

"Darwin, what we're doing here is the fulfillment of a dream, a dream for you, me, and thousands of other people."

Darwin was seated in his listening mode. Walt was standing by with a display portfolio. Townshend was pacing, gesturing, and posturing, a Madison Avenue version of Mick Jagger.

"This is a special place. You know it better than anyone. This is the frontier. It was the frontier for the Indians who came east from China; it was the frontier for the English; and it was the frontier for those of us who escaped suburbia. The roots of adventure are deep within this rocky soil, and it's time the world knew about it.

"This plan has been in the works for years. And it wasn't my idea. It was Bruce's vision. I'm hoping he will come back to share it."

Darwin shifted uncomfortably. Bruce Liebermann, the Stowe Stallion, left Upper Granville a year earlier, when he split with his wife, Françoise. He left behind a number of burned bridges. He had also left Darwin with the knowledge that he had conducted an affair with Sue Clarke. Darwin had never spoken of the matter with either Sue or Townshend. He did not know if either of them knew that the Stallion had taken him into his confidence. Indeed, Darwin did not know whether Townshend knew of his wife's indiscretions. In any case, it was squirming time.

"I doubt that will happen," continued Townshend. "This was his dream, a complete restoration of this village the way it was when Hiram Blanchard came down here from Baddeck, Nova Scotia, and built it into a thriving frontier town. This house was a tavern. There was a saw mill, a dance hall, a general store, a stagecoach stop. Upper Granville was a bustling outpost. But you know all this. It's all there in Alton Blanchard's book."

"What's the program, Townshend? Where's the beef?"

"Darwin, we give you '1839,' an authentic recreation of a New England pioneer town." On this cue Walt Gunion opened the portfolio and commenced his spiel.

" 'Eighteen thirty-nine' is the first project of Preservation Trust (United States), Inc. We call it 'Trust U.S.' The company exists to bring American history to life, while at the same time bringing life to American history. That's our slogan: 'History to life, and life to history.' " Walt flipped past the title page to a topographical map of the Upper Granville Valley. Darwin saw his house with the note, "Tavern, privately owned."

The presentation took almost forty-five minutes. Walt and Townshend led Darwin through a series of renditions done by a Boston architect firm and financial plans blessed by Burlington's top CPA outfit.

While the town was to be living history, there were no such lofty historical ambitions for the accommodations necessary to house the hordes. The hillside where Walt's house now perched was destined to become a bank of luxury condominiums with an eighteen-hole golf course. The access road down to Route 100 would be widened to four lanes and paved. When Walt and Townshend finally stopped for air, Darwin scarcely knew where to begin.

"I must say, I'm impressed. There's a fortune in presentation materials alone. How did you do it without anyone noticing?"

"You can understand," answered Walt, "how a program like this can be scuttled in its early stages by bad publicity. That's why we did not want to come public until all the t's were crossed and i's dotted.

"And I'll tell you the truth, Darwin. We're taking you into our confidence before anyone else. You know more about this than our wives. Sue knows I've been working with Walt on something, but she thinks it has to do with buying a wood lot."

"This plan will cost millions!" exclaimed Darwin.

"Seventy-nine point eight million for phase one alone," said Townshend matter-of-factly.

"And you guys have that kind of money?"

Neither answered, but their steady looks were enough for affirmation.

"You guys want another beer?" Darwin asked.

The beer break was enough to derail the Trust U.S. express momentarily. When the men settled back into their chairs, Darwin felt enough like a peer and neighbor to try some more acute probing:

"It's a great idea, but it's got two Achilles' heels. The first is that you don't own the land."

"Not all of it. Not yet. But more than you think. We've been acquiring every piece that has come on the market for the last two years. We trust that ultimately everyone will have the common sense to be ruled by their own economic self-interest."

"Did that business with Bennett and the stake have something to do with all this?"

"Yes," said Townshend. He and Walt looked at each other conspiratorially and laughed. "Bennett doesn't know what's going on yet, but he's figured out that something's happening. He has been looking to expand the farm, and yet every direction he turns, we've already been there. He never owned the land on that hillside. A cousin of his did, and we bought it from him. Then our lawyers sent Bennett a letter to get off."

"Nice guys," said Darwin. "So are you here to make an offer I can't refuse on this place?"

"Our public announcement of 1839 comes in one month. We'll be flying in press from New York, Boston, and all over. By that time we will want to feel secure in our commitments on the individual properties. Your place is key. This is the tavern. And you're a key, as well. The others will follow your lead." Townshend displayed complete confidence in his pronouncements.

"And we will be more than generous in our offers," chimed in Walt.

"What about the Blanchards? Dairy farming is their religion. No one's going to tell them to leave."

"Darwin," condescended Townshend, "the Blanchards aren't dumb. They know that the twentieth century is here. With the money we'll give them, they can buy themselves the finest operation in the state, or they can sip piña coladas on a tropical island forever. It's not as if they are making a killing in dairy farming now. They're barely squeaking by. We're not taking anything away from them; we're giving opportunity. We're just counting on the fact that, ultimately, we're all slaves to our own economic self-interest."

"Yeah, yeah. You said that before. Townshend, you've come a long way in a short time, but I'm not sure I like where you're at. Walt's always been a fool, but you're catching up real fast."

Walt blustered, but Townshend maintained his cool under fire. "Darwin, this is why we talked to you first. Taking people's houses touches on deep emotions, no matter how sensitive and generous we are. We appreciate that. But, also understand that ultimately we want to protect this valley from becoming the Appalachian backwater that so many similar towns have become. This is one of the few remaining unspoiled small towns. It's a piece of art that we are trying to save and to share."

"Okay," said Darwin, "let's suppose I trust you. There's another flaw in your plan. Why would anyone come here? There's no skiing, no lake. It's just country. If there was a reason for the masses to come here, they would have come decades ago."

Townshend's face twisted into a smile of smug-faced

satisfaction. Checkmate, he seemed to say. He looked at Walt, whose face was suddenly a visual chortle. "Go ahead, Walt," said Townshend, "tell him about Dairy World."

Walt produced another blueprint, this one depicting a large, outdoor amphitheater. "You said this place was just country, Darwin. We all feel that way, but it's only because we can't see the forest for the trees. We take for granted things that are quite exceptional—"

"Especially if properly positioned and marketed," interjected Townshend.

"Welcome to Dairy World," said Walt with a flourish. "A fourteen-thousand-seat facility that will do for the cow what Sea World did for the dolphin. Did you know that cows are actually smarter than killer whales? And isn't it a coincidence that they are both black and white?

"We are almost equidistant from Boston, New York, and Montreal, with a combined metropolitan population of more than twenty million."

"This is our trump card with Bennett Blanchard," chimed in Townshend. "If his emotional ties are so great that he is blind to the economics of our generosity, then we plan to offer him a job running the Dairy World stables. He'll be working with prize stock from all over the world."

"Of course, we'd prefer to just buy him out, though," said Walt. "I think he'd be a pain in the ass to work with."

Darwin's eyes turned into silent Black & Deckers, drilling three-eighths-inch holes in Walt's skull. "And what bone are you planning to toss me? Do I get to wear a silly costume while serving overpriced drinks to tourists in the tavern?"

There was silence, a natural ending point. Finally, Townshend added the sign-off:

"Darwin, we're not asking any commitment at this time, only for you to have an open mind and to learn more about what we're trying to do and how it involves you. We're neighbors and friends. You've known us for years. We're asking you to trust us, but not blindly. Just don't get your hackles up so much that you don't even allow us to deliver our message."

"Okay," said Darwin, finishing his beer and standing to signal an end to the visit. "I'll listen, because this is the craziest thing I've seen since the first time I saw *Monty Python's Flying Circus*. But don't either of you think for a second that I am approving or in any way going along with what you are proposing. Where I stand, right now —me, Darwin Hunter, the great Butt Kicker—is that I think you can both go kick yourselves."

Only he did not say "kick."

5

Captain Goo-Roo, or Darwin Does ARFO

"Every person in this room is a mover and shaker."
Townshend Clarke IV handed Darwin a drink.

"What's this?" asked Darwin.

"A highball."

"A highball? That's a grown-up drink. Can't I have a beer?"

"You can't drink beer at a function like this," lectured Townshend. "It's too déclassé."

"If that means 'having no class whatsoever,' then beer's the drink for me."

"Look," said Walt Gunion with a nudge, "there's Dunwoody." He gestured with his eyes across the banquet room of Nino's Nook. Linwood "Woody" Dunwoody looked to be in his early fifties, a robust man with a logger's hands (but no ring on his wienie) and a ruddy face as creased as the terrain surrounding Center Granville. A group of five or six men circled the politician, their respective body postures acknowledging his dominance.

Townshend spoke to Darwin out of the side of his

mouth. "I'll introduce you, but if it gets into anything political, don't be surprised if I distance myself. I can't afford to be on this guy's bad side."

"Townshend, you are such a fucking hypocrite. When they shaved your head they must have scraped your brain. We've been neighbors for nine years. You don't have to be ashamed of me," protested Darwin.

"Get real. I'm sure he's heard of your intention to enter the race. I'm sure he knows it's a joke, but maybe his sense of humor isn't too good. You hear what I'm saying?"

"Maybe," Walt let his chortles telegraph a punchline, "he's afraid you'll kick butt."

"I can't believe I let you morons talk me into this."

The second Sunday of every month marks the gathering at Nino's Nook of the Central Vermont Chapter of the Grand Order of ARFO. Important men collect to promote fellowship and community service amidst an environment of cigar smoke, highballs, and rubber chicken.

ARFO is an acronym for Affiliated Rural Fraternal Organizations. The organization was founded by Leominster (pronounced Lemon-stir) Terry in 1949. It was just after the Big One, and the nation's males were joining fraternal organizations in droves to maintain that sense of camaraderie that had developed during what Terry referred to as "the ultimate deer camp," World War II. At the time Granville had chapters for VFW, Odd Fellows, Kiwanis, Jaycees, Moose, Grange, Rotary, Shriners . . . everything but the Raccoon Club. The problem was, even with every male between the ages of seventeen and death belonging to three organizations, none of the groups could muster the critical mass to survive.

Leominster Terry proposed the creation of a fraternal organization geared toward the needs of the thinly populated, and ARFO was born. As with other organizations, this club was long on symbols and ritual and short on purpose. Terry, who then ran the only store in Granville to sell men's clothing, designed the uniforms himself, as well as creating the memorable slogan, "Our Friends are ARFOs." He wrote the club song, the club pledge, the club charter, and the club franchising agreement. He created the club rituals and established the ranking of officers that is used to this day. But though the ARFO concept worked well for Granville, no other communities embraced the charter.

Darwin knew he had made a mistake within moments of climbing into the leather folds of Townshend's Lincoln. He had never trusted Walt, and now that Townshend had his mind on the grandiose conversion of Upper Granville into a theme park, he trusted him less. Still, Darwin acquiesced, convinced by the two men—as well as Sammi —that if he seriously held political aspirations, he needed to better understand the private side of public life.

Darwin had not yet formalized his candidacy, but because of his relative prominence as a doctor, author, and now a television star, everyone knew of his interest. No one, however—not his wife, not his neighbors, not Woody Dunwoody—yet took him seriously.

"Hello, Darwin, glad you could join us." Dunwoody's pedigree was purest Chuck, yet he exuded the blind confidence of Flatlander facing his first mud season. "So you're the man who would be king. What's this I hear about you wanting to put me in the unemployment line?"

"That's it," said Darwin. "I wanna kick your butt."

There was a split second of silence, long enough for Townshend Clarke's life to flash before him. Woody Dunwoody returned, "Forget about 'king.' How about 'court jester'?" He then sucked in a deep breath to power a belly laugh that shook Nino's and signaled all within earshot that hysterics were appropriate. There was no rejoinder, only a tapering off of the laughter that left the focus clearly in Dunwoody's court.

"Well," he started wiping the corners of his eyes as if there really were tears of mirth present, "politics is a horse race. A real horse race." Darwin had to hand it to him, his timing was exquisite. Everyone was hanging on Dunwoody's every syllable, and by now he had managed to draw another fifteen people into the arena:

"But I can't see why anyone would enter with a dead horse."

Pandemonium.

Even Darwin chuckled, giving a master his due. Dunwoody put a friendly, but shackling, hand on Darwin's neck and offered to buy him a drink. Okay, said Darwin, but it's gotta be a beer. Dunwoody got a beer for himself as well. The next time Darwin looked, both Walt and Townshend were holding bottles of Budweiser.

"Seriously, Darwin, we've got to think this through." Dunwoody guided him away from the crowd, creating an island of intimacy in the sea of humanity.

"You can't possibly be threatened by the fact that I may run against you?"

"By you? Never. But let me tell you a fact of political life. The more horses in the field, the more chance someone will fall in some shit. For me, the real enemy is Weinstein. Now, she's a legitimate opponent who offers the electorate a clear choice—they can have one of their own kind, or a bulldykeflatlanderhebe. What muddies the issue is when you little guys get in the race. First you come in and tie up the lunatic fringe vote. Now there's talk of Mimi

Cox—Earle Cox the banker's wife—declaring. She'll tie up the do-gooder vote. Do you know her?"

Darwin shook his head.

"What a wasted piece of human flesh. She's got a neck longer'n my arm. That's the only way it can reach her asshole. Anyway, Darwin, my point is, you little guys are like pimples on the face of democracy. Ignore you and pretty soon you'll go away, but while you're there you can make things kinda ugly. So why don't we skip the spotted-mirror stage? You tell me what you're looking for in this shootin' match, and I'll try to give it to you. We can both live very happily in this district."

Darwin tightened his lips slightly. The man was clearly corrupt and a bigot, but at least he was direct. Darwin was impressed. His reply ("I'll have to think on it") was thoughtful, more than lame.

"You do that," Dunwoody boomed, emphasizing with his fist. "You're okay, Darwin. I'll give you a little taste of political life tonight, but keep in mind there's lots more where that comes from. Nothing personal." He pumped Darwin's hand again before turning back to his legion of admirers.

Dunwoody was both a Grand Bowser (an ARFian rank of distinction), as well as the evening's recipient of Man of the Year. Darwin could not quite catch the drift of the predinner ceremony. There were a few songs with barking noises followed by a pledge of allegiance that mentioned Leominster Terry four times and deer hunting twice. And, finally, some mumbo-jumbo including slapping oneself on each side of the cheek and holding one's breath for almost a minute. There was a recounting of the organization's glorious history by Leominster's son, Leominster, culminating with salute to the ARFO mascot, the mongrel.

The slogan of "Our Friends are ARFOs" impressed Townshend and Walt. With their grand plans for 1839, they were encountering the first glimmerings of institutional clout. They interpreted the slogan as meaning that any obstinacy within the community would be overcome by encounters on ARFian fields.

"After you've gotten shitfaced with someone," said Walt, "it's tougher to say no."

Townshend even mentioned to Darwin that he would not be surprised, several years hence, if he and Walt followed in Dunwoody's footsteps as Men of the Year.

Coffee was served, along with a vanilla pudding that Darwin knew even his kids would not eat. The reigning Bowser Poobah of ARFO introduced Dunwoody, who took the stage to warm applause. The first thing Dunwoody did was to ask Darwin to stand. Even though Darwin was still unofficial, Dunwoody said with a between-you-and-me wink, this was a man likely to share the ballot with him and Natalie Weinstein. He welcomed this "nipple sucker" (the ARFian term for an uninitiated recruit) with warmth, eloquence, and flourish.

Dunwoody then explained, while Darwin stood and fidgeted uncomfortably, how this challenge was no more than the latest assault on his single-handed defense of all that was decent about America. In the course of coffee and vanilla pudding, Dunwoody managed to single out each group that threatened this way of life.

Darwin was not sure which of the groups lambasted by the senator included him. Probably not women, Dallas Cowboy fans, Jews, Iranian terrorists, or Negroes, but undoubtedly communists, faggots, Flatlanders, and fools. With the exception of Flatlanders and fools, none of the other minorities were tolerated as members of ARFO.

Dunwoody left to a standing ovation. Darwin was simply left standing. Later, he scraped self-consciously at the bottom of his pudding dish, thankful that the group had not stoned him. Finally, it ended. Darwin breathed a sigh of relief and asked Townshend if he was ready to go.

"Leave? Are you crazy? This is the best part. This is where we bond. This is what it's all about, Darwin. You'd be amazed at the deals that go down here. Hey, how 'bout that Dunwoody being so gracious with you?"

Townshend was so fixated on cutting the amazing deal that he absentmindedly surrendered to Darwin the keys to the Lincoln. As he walked into the parking lot of Nino's, another burst of male hilarity could be heard behind him. Mr. Linwood "Woody" Dunwoody had struck yet another responsive chord.

The parking lot was a still life of early December. The ground was covered until April. The air was crisp; the ski areas would all be making snow tonight. Jupiter hung in the western horizon, the brightest point in an electric sky. Darwin paused to reflect.

"Our Friends are ARFOs," he said to Jupiter. "Give me a fucking break."

He had escaped without thinking through his next step. It was only eight-thirty, too late to catch the kids before bed and yet too early to come home without facing an inquisition from Sammi. He had just decided where he did not want to be; all he needed now was an acceptable alternative.

"When in doubt," said Darwin, unlocking the Lincoln, "drive."

One half hour later Darwin was seated on a bar stool at the Club 100, just south of Montpelier. The club itself was an unattractive building, a Quonset hut set on the outskirts of the state capital. Darwin had driven by the club many times but had never felt the urge to stop, his bar-hanging days mostly behind him, gone the way of his former hairline. He had always been intrigued by a sign that read LIVE FOR THE 342ND CONSECUTIVE SUNDAY, CAPTAIN GOO-ROO, THE ONE MANN JAM! Each week the number would be crossed out and increased by one.

The Captain's one man rock-and-roll extravaganza had been playing almost since Darwin's first days in Vermont. He was as much a part of the Vermont scene as lost leaf peepers or jumper cables. For years Darwin had been meaning to go. As an ex rock and roller himself, he was curious. Tonight's early exit from the ARFO meeting provided the perfect opportunity.

Darwin knew little about the Captain, only that his real name was Billy Mann, that he had a late-night rock-and-roll show on a Montpelier radio station that did not make it as far as Upper Granville, and that his specialty was in getting the audience to sing along with oldies but goldies.

The Club 100 was bag balm for the nerve endings exposed at the ARFO meeting. The all-male atmosphere, the good ol' boy gregariousness of Dunwoody, the illusion of propriety, formed an environment at once false and threatening. By contrast, the tacky atmosphere of the club offered real people and real beer. There were no more than fifteen people present, apparently regulars, but Darwin, the obvious outsider, felt no hostility. They sipped beer and chatted, mostly oblivious to the manic performance of the man on stage.

Not Darwin. He was enthralled by Captain Goo-Roo, who wove a pathway through the catacombs of rock and roll, taking along anyone who cared to go. After watching a full hour of songs either written by, performed by, or about anyone named Jimmy, Darwin was convinced that he was in the presence of one of the geniuses of the twentieth century.

"This guy is amazing," Darwin bubbled to the bartender, offering his glass back for a refill.

"If by that," said the bartender, a taciturn type with a beard that had not seen scissors in a decade, "you mean he's an asshole, then I'd have to agree." He used the word asshole as an endearment; it connoted familiarity, not contempt.

"I'm talking about his musical ability." The bartender returned a brimming glass. "And I'm talking about his position in life. Billy Mann is an open wound. His wife has left him, his son has cancer, he's in debt up to his eyeballs, and his car needs a new alternator. The guy needs a life transplant. But he never complains. Instead he knocks himself out playing for fifteen people on Sunday nights. And most of them are ignoring him."

Captain Goo-Roo's between-song patter repeated the intimate details of a painful life, though without a trace of self-pity, leading thematically to the next tune. Somewhere in the pain, the Captain found innocence; in the frustration, exuberance; and in the smallest detail of life, rock and roll.

Billy Mann gave a progress report on his lifelong ambition to create a Foundation for the Preservation of Rock and Roll, headquartered in Montpelier. That week he had sent out more than fifty letters to various record companies, producers, and artists. He read some of the replies, each a study in condescension. After two or three, any sense of embarrassment was gone, and the audience was in stitches at the supercilious hypocrisy that big stars and big companies used to tell a little guy in Vermont that they did not take him seriously. Billy led the laughter, then started playing a string of songs having to do with money, beginning with "First I Look at the Purse."

The bartender caught Darwin grinning broadly at the manic performance. He permitted himself a small chuckle, just a little snort. "Like I say, Billy Mann is a piece of work."

" 'Quite a rigging,' as the farmer in my town would say. Do you think I could meet him?" asked Darwin.

"It's more a question of could you avoid it?" came the bartender's cryptic reply. Sensing that he had been too obtuse, he backtracked: "Everyone knows Billy Mann by the end of the night."

"Will you introduce me?"

The bartender looked at Darwin as if he had asked whether or not he could cut wind. "Introductions aren't necessary. Just don't be shy. When he starts jamming, be front and center. He knows you're here. Just listen closely. He'll get around to you."

Darwin did not have to wait long. Billy Mann did two more money songs, then went right into one called "Stranger in Town," followed by several others based loosely around the theme of strangers. In between songs he kept up a running monologue that Darwin gradually recognized was directed to him.

"People are strange, when they are strangers," said Billy as he pulled off his acoustic guitar and settled himself at a rickety spinet piano. "Reminds me of a tune. But there are no strangers at the Club 100, just Captain Goo-Roo and his minions of fans, most of whom have stayed home tonight to watch a made-for-TV Sunday night movie. It's a great one about a young virgin who contracts a terrible disease and spends nearly two agonizing hours hanging on through six thousand commercials before croaking just in time for the eleven o'clock news.

"So he wants to meet me. Hah, you and every good-looking girl in Central Vermont. I know. Reminds me of a tune, but then, so does just about everything. Why does he want to meet me? Maybe this is it. Springsteen's manager up here for a holiday, stops in at a local roadhouse and can't believe that he's discovered a national treasure."

"Nah," came a voice from the darkness. "You probably owe him money."

Captain Goo-Roo laughed and played some aimless chords. "You're right. The man obviously doesn't know that the Captain doesn't take breaks, so if one wants to meet the Captain, one comes to him, preferably bearing a gift, a libation, a big, cold wet one. The bartender knows what the Captain drinks."

Darwin looked to the bartender, who had already set a beer by his elbow. "Now you've met Captain Goo-Roo," he said simply. Darwin grabbed his own beer, plus one for the Captain, and moved down to a table by the small stage where the Captain performed.

They chatted in between songs. Billy Mann was thinner than Darwin, roughly the same age. Their faces told of different lives: Darwin's of prep schools, the Midwest, Dartmouth, medical school; the Captain's of fishing boats, sidewalks, late nights, and sleazy bars. Their lives intersected at rock and roll, Darwin having once played for Cincinnati's hottest teen band (circa 1965), Run for Your Coats. During the same era Billy Mann toiled for a similar band in Rhode Island, Gary and the Gang Green. Now they challenged each other to recall trivia from their adolescence.

The Captain was unstumpable, yet he had never been

so creatively extended during his seven-year tenure at Club 100. He had to dredge songs from the recesses of his gray matter, occasionally needing the newcomer's help on lyrics and chord progressions. He dragged Darwin on stage more than once. Although the doctor's musical skills had deteriorated as badly as his high school French, he performed with the gusto of a man getting a one-night reprieve to his youth.

As the night wore on, the One Mann Jam side of the Captain's billing became clear. One by one patrons were lured stageside where they were willingly provoked into participation. Tables became drums, beer bottles basses, and hands castanets. Everyone sang, following the Captain's orders. Darwin was amazed. Behind the Captain's lead, this ragtag collection of Vermonters became a band that compensated with spontaneity and enthusiasm for what it lacked in discipline. Whenever the spirit flagged, there was Billy Mann mounting another charge, rallying the troops around the Everly Brothers, the Beatles, or some other fallen hero from rock and roll's past.

For Darwin the success of the night was made even sweeter by its juxtaposition with the ARFO meeting. He had never met a more compelling leader than Captain Goo-Roo. Even though Darwin had switched to ice water hours before, he felt drunk with his discovery of the Captain.

Jake, the bartender, shouted out last call. The Captain ended the music and strolled to the bar, where Darwin bought him another beer.

"What do you do after a show?" asked Darwin.

"Go home. Start working on next week's show," answered Billy. "How about you?"

"Just go home," said Darwin. "Wanna come? I'll show

you my collection of Elvis memorabilia plus the piece of the fuselage from the plane in which Buddy Holly crashed and burned." The Captain nodded without hesitation.

"Maybe you'll donate them to the Foundation."

They drove to Upper Granville, Darwin promising to drive Billy Mann home in the morning. Darwin babbled, a departure from his normal counterpunching style. He told Mann about the ARFO meeting, his twelve biographies of Elvis, his relationship with Sammi, his plans for the Senate, his kids. They arrived at the Hunter household and sat in Darwin's study, sipping from his collection of Scotches as he continued his life story, his opinion of Janis Joplin, Townshend's plan for the valley, and the intrinsic differences between Flatlanders and Chucks.

The Captain did not talk much, having become depleted during his nonstop four-hour performance, but he nodded and murmured. Through his silence and sympathy, Darwin concluded this was the wisest man he had ever met. At times their conversation was so lucid, it was as if the words were etched on a glass brick:

Darwin: I want to run for the Senate because I want to give something to a society that has given me a lot.
Captain: That's why I play rock and roll.
Darwin: Rock and roll is such a pure form of expression.
Captain: Pure as Del Shannon's falsetto in "Runaway."
Darwin: Exactly. We played that in my band.
Captain: Your band and every other band since 1963.
Darwin: You know, you and I are a lot alike. We both want to be rich, famous, and immortal, only you've been true to your art, while I sold out.
Captain: And now you're making up for lost time.
Darwin: Exactly! I hadn't realized that, but it's true.

The men listened to scratchy albums that had not been played in more than twenty years but which had been dutifully lugged from place to place to make possible just such an evening as this. Darwin got blankets and pillows for the Captain, but it was he who fell asleep first. Billy stayed up and grooved to music until four.

They awoke jaggedly when the alarms went off and the kids descended. Darwin arose from the floor, stiffer than a starched collar and feeling that all the soft tissue between his joints had disappeared. He did not groan, however, but rather smiled, even as he looked into Sammi's face, a face that conveyed rage and puzzlement as she eyed the stranger on the floor.

"Good morning, darling," said Darwin, wondering how he could feel so great and so terrible at the same time. "I'd like you to meet Captain Goo-Roo, my campaign manager."

6

North Country Samurai

"Get him out of here," hissed Sammi. She turned before Darwin had a chance to respond. The Captain struggled to rise like a boxer trying to beat the count, and careened back down into a heap.

"I keep forgetting I'm too old for this," said Darwin.

"Why are we waking up?" asked Billy. "It's barely morning."

"I should have told you," said Darwin. "When I'm not being a late-night raconteur and all-around bon vivant, I'm a normal person who works for a living and yells at the kids every ten minutes to finish their breakfasts."

"I've been there," said Billy, rubbing his eyes while changing course. "I don't think your old lady likes me."

"Don't worry about her," said Darwin, finally achieving an upright position and surveying the den. Yes, he admitted, it did look a little messy, a fraternity room, perhaps, but not Animal House. "I'll handle her."

He marched to the kitchen, where Sammi was broadcasting her displeasure by making percussion instruments of the kitchen appliances. Darwin stood silently as she slammed the refrigerator door, turned on the blender, and set juice glasses on the table with the precision of rifle shots. He was the first to speak:

"Let's sell tickets to this one."

"What?"

"Let's sell tickets to this fight, because it's bound to last longer than Tyson-Spinks, and it will probably be bloodier. We can try to get the black guy with the electric hair to put it on closed circuit—"

"That's right, Darwin. Make a joke of it, just like every-thing in life."

"What is there to be upset about? Is someone hurt? Have we lost money?"

"You stay out all night. Drive home drunk, dragging this low-life into our home, and I'm supposed to be un-derstanding?"

"You're way off base, and I welcome the opportunity to set the record straight, but not now. In the eighteen years we've been married I have never once brought home an uninvited guest. Now, for the first time, I have, and I want him treated as a guest. Let's save the spit and venom for when I get home, but for now let's have the dignity to act like civilized people."

"You're a great one to talk about civilized—"

Darwin cut her off, his voice taking on its best dominant-male edge: "Look, when I get home, we can fight with knives, guns, and words. We can do it in private, in front of the kids, or invite over the whole neighborhood. We can go five rounds or fifteen. You set the rules. But I'm setting this rule—no fighting now. There are kids to get off to school, stoves to be stoked, and a guest—a friend of mine—to be fed. Let's do it."

The uneasy truce was established, but tension blanketed the breakfast table. The kids were initially shy with the stranger, but Billy's natural affinity toward children soon prevailed. He was "Uncle Captain" by the time the school bus came. Sammi wore her indignation like a festering sore on the end of her nose, throwing bran muffins at the men as she would Milk Bones to General Beauregard. Darwin chattered about his experiences at the ARFO meeting the previous evening but drew little response other than the Captain's muttered, "Reminds me of a tune."

Darwin drove Billy back to his modest apartment in the rear of what was once the Main Street Cinema in downtown Montpelier. Billy bought the derelict building with the hope of one day making it the headquarters for the Foundation for the Preservation of Rock and Roll.

"What needs preserving about rock and roll?" asked Darwin as the Captain led him on a tour through the dusty seats and rheumy woodwork of the small but once-elegant theater. "Rock and roll is here to stay."

"Reminds me of a tune," said the Captain. "It's like anything precious. While you have it, when you're glorying in the midst of it, you take it for granted. Then one day it's gone, usually forever."

"But this nostalgia craze—"

"I'm not talking nostalgia!" He spat the word with such vehemence that Darwin was taken aback. "I'm talking preservation. I'm not talking warm, fuzzy memories; I'm talking a culture's struggle to communicate. I'm not talking K-Tel's *Great Hits from the Fabulous Fifties*; I'm talking cave paintings, Stonehenge, and Brian Wilson singing 'Surfer Girl.' "

There was silence in the theater, a silence filled with

meaning, as Darwin suddenly understood the dream of Billy Mann.

The doctor went through a routine day of appointments, prescriptions, and paperwork. Then it was dinner (baked chicken, brussel sprouts, and baked potato), homework, bedtime stories, and finally that moment of silence.

The bell sounded: fight time.

"Let us begin," began Darwin. Sammi was doing last-minute Christmas shopping in the Horchow catalogue, but closed it, saving her place with a finger. "First of all, I wasn't out all night. In fact I wasn't much later than I would have been had I stayed at that ridiculous ARFO meeting. 'Our Friends are ARFOs.' You would have puked.

"Secondly, I switched to club soda by ten o'clock, so I wasn't driving drunk, and third, if I do something un-usual, like bring home a new friend, you should assume the best, not the worst, and act accordingly."

"Darwin." Her voice made his name carry a bewildering array of emotions. "You're weird. You should have mar-ried someone weird."

"Oh, you're weird, too, honey. Don't sell yourself short."

She almost smiled. "Tired? Yes. Bored? Absolutely. Weird? No. I know you can't really help yourself. There was a good article about men like you in *The Professional Woman*. You've got what is known as the Peter Pan Syn-drome, and you'll never grow up. I've got to learn to accept that."

"Who would ever want to grow up?"

"Most people would, and most people do. I have, for instance. I've had my youth, I've had my children, I have my home. Now I'm looking to make my own small contribution to society. I donate my energies to organizations that I think are worthy. I try to improve myself. I've found an inspirational model in Natalie Weinstein, but I'm realistic, perhaps resigned to the amount of influence any individual can have."

Sammi returned to the world of Horchow. Darwin pretended to read the *Christian Science Monitor* for a few minutes, basking in the relative peace and harmony, then breaking it:

"I have a plan."

"God help us," murmured Sammi without looking up.

Darwin explained. If he was to lead, and he felt this to be his destiny, it was important that he be able to focus. He could not stomach the Linwood "Woody" Dunwoody approach, a good ol' boy network that assured prosperity for the few. No, Darwin Hunter would stand for equality and opportunity. His style would be to lead by example, engendering confidence via the purity and openness of his own actions.

He stood and paced. This was the greatest challenge of his life. And he had to approach it seriously, methodically, the same way he approached medical school and training for his first marathon.

For months now he had wrestled with his own motivations. Was he serious about becoming a public servant? Or was he interested in running for State Senate for egotistical reasons? Now he knew the answer. He wanted to run, and moreover, he wanted to serve. In Gimp he had found a political advisor, in Billy Mann an inspirational leader. What he needed now was to prepare himself for a race, to undertake a crash course to ready himself to take on opponents who were already far ahead of him. This competition was somewhere between a game and a war.

He would conduct it as the former, but prepare for the latter. He would be a warrior, flying the pennants of his constituency. He would become a North Country Samurai.

Sammi put down her catalogue and removed his glasses. "Darwin, one thing I thought I could count on is that you would not become a religious freak. But you sound suspiciously like someone on cable television on Sunday morning. Next, you'll be asking me to send money."

No, said Darwin. There comes a time, however, when one must be willing to lay theory aside and to demonstrate action.

"I have been hoping," said his wife, "that this political thing is like a pimple, very obvious and ugly for a while, but temporary."

How strange, thought Darwin, that my wife is choosing the same analogy as my opponent to describe my political ambitions.

Sammi continued, "I hoped that the ARFO meeting might be a jolt of reality, but instead I wake up to find a hairy kook sleeping on the floor. Darwin, you are a forty-year-old eye doctor with three children and a demanding wife. Act like an adult; give up this crazy idea."

"I promise not to shortchange you or the children. My practice will suffer a bit, but it's not as if the collective eyesight of Central Vermont will suffer because I'm in the office less. I can do it, Sammi. And Billy's going to be my campaign manager."

"Captain Goo-Roo?" She pronounced the name as if holding a slug in her mouth.

"Yes."

"You're serious? You're going to run for a political office for which you have no qualifications, and your campaign will be run by a broken-down hippie guitar player?"

"Yes, I will be a senator, but I'll still be a doctor, and a husband, a father, a jogger, an ex rock-and-roll star, and, in the eyes of the Bennett Blanchards of the world, a flaming douche bag."

"Bennett won't be alone." Sammi took a deep breath, then gave reality one final try. "Darwin, it's very hard for me to support you in an effort I regard as total buffoonery. And as far as Natalie Weinstein is concerned, you're putting us on opposite sides of the fence."

"I love you, and I'll need your support, especially as I get into the execution of my plan," said Darwin, going over to the woodstove and stoking it with two logs. "But I want you to vote for Weinstein if you think she's the better candidate. This is America. That's what this race is all about!

"I know I have not followed the standard path to a political career—that's why I think I will be a better leader. But first I have to cleanse myself. I have to start from a zero base. I have to start by untangling things, and I have to start with myself."

"What are you going to do?" asked Sammi. Her tone was of trepidation more than curiosity. She was expecting anything. She wondered if she still knew this ball of energy pacing around her kitchen.

Darwin laid out his plan. After the holidays he would move out from the house to the sauna for the month of January. He would eschew all forms of stimulants and intoxicants, even beer! He would drink only distilled water; he would eat only brown rice and lime juice; he would follow an exercise regimen; he would chant.

Sammi began sobbing softly. Her Horchow catalogue fell to the floor. Darwin came over to comfort her. "Don't worry, baby," he said, "I'm not changing. This is a phase, a very conscious phase that I need to get me to the point where I can make this plan work. I have to be in shape physically, mentally, and spiritually, and I need you for it to happen. I don't want your vote, just your support."

He touched her softly on the shoulder. She slapped his hand away.

The personal tensions gradually diminished in the groundswell of emotions that surround Christmas. They did not disappear completely, as shown by an incident on Christmas Eve. Darwin was running late. Besides a full day at the office, he had made appearances at two Christmas parties—one at Central Vermont Hospital, the other at the Club 100. A third, for the Upper Granville community, was scheduled at the Pisanos'. Darwin called Sammi, told her he was running late and that he would meet her and the kids there. Hurry up, she said, because you're playing Santa and we all have to be at the church service by eight. And don't forget the costume; it's under our bed.

He drove home at ninety miles an hour and began tearing off clothes and putting on the costume. The red suit was seventy-five sizes too big, putting Darwin into complete panic. He got a stapler from his desk and began the tailoring equivalent of chain-saw carpentry.

From outside came the persistent barking of Emil Dummerston Weed's hound, Maggie May. Due to his already agitated state, this noise grated on Darwin as if he had crying babies strapped to each shoulder. He found that by yelling at the dog he could buy a few moments of silence. As time passed and his deadline grew nearer, the dog's barking grated more heavily and Darwin's expletives became both more frequent and more explicit.

Unbeknownst to Darwin, Hannah had arranged for the choir of Upper Granville Congregationalist Church to come to town for a round of candlelight caroling. At this moment they were assembled in front of the Hunter household, and (a-one and-a two and-a three) were two notes into "Silent Night" when the front door burst open and a man half clad in a Santa Claus suit shouted at the top of his lungs:

"FUCK YOU AND THE HORSE YOU RODE IN ON!"

The door slammed shut. After several minutes of embarrassed confusion Hannah convinced the choir to try once more. Unfortunately, Emil's dog had begun baying, bringing Darwin to the front door for another epithet just as the group reached the word town in "O Little Town of Bethlehem":

"SHUT UP YOU FUCKING MANGY ASSHOLE!"

Again the door slammed shut, Darwin oblivious to his audience. Hannah decided to preserve whatever was left of the holiday spirit by moving up the road. Only when the choir encountered a more jovial Darwin Claus at the Pisanos' was the matter straightened out.

Darwin's month as a North Country Samurai began at the stroke of midnight on January first, at the Hunters' traditional New Year's Eve theme party. This year's theme was "Ethan Allen's New Year." The home was dancing in candlelight, a roaring blaze in the fireplace, by the side of which Darwin concocted foaming colonial punches with fittingly colorful names—Abbot's Flip, Calibogus, and Whistlestop. Townshend Clarke came in an outfit of leather breeches and ruffled shirt that, but for his shaved head and earrings, took a page from the book of colonial Vermont. Walt Gunion was identically bedecked, revealing that he and Townshend commissioned the outfits in preparation for the formal ribbon cutting for 1839.

Stella Blanchard brought loaves of bread from an old family recipe, with crust as thick as turtle shells and moist gummy innards that turned butter, cheese, and slices of onion into a banquet. Walt, forgetting for a moment that he was not bonding at an ARFO gathering, got so excited that he started babbling to her about franchise rights. Stella, who shared the community's skepticism about the planned development of the valley, returned Walt's questions with a sweet smile, slicing and handing him yet another piece of bread to keep his mouth full and voice quiet.

Howard "Warren" Pease, his store closed for the night, spewed massive doses of historical trivia about Ethan Allen, colonial drinking customs, and the land-grant covenants between the Crown and early land barons. Most of his knowledge had been gained that day from a piece of computer software called MacColonial History. Howard networked with fellow Macintosh fiends and had it sent up via modem from Georgia, just in time for New Year's.

Darwin, noticing Hannah Duncan's eyes becoming opaque and rolling back into her head under the onslaught of Warren's nonstop barrage of minutiae, asked, "How can a guy make such fascinating information a total bore?"

"You've heard people described as 'the life of the party'?" retorted Hannah. "This guy's the Black Death."

Emil Dummerston Weed stuck to Genesee rather than Darwin's foaming creations. Emil had with him his new love, Deneice Moss, known universally as Sunny. Physically, she was as close to square as a human being can be, measuring four-foot-eight by four-foot-eight.

This was the first time Emil had gone public with his new girlfriend, an event of significance in a valley where one's romantic life is considered community property. Emil was at a critical juncture. Now in his late thirties, he needed to find a life companion or resign himself to a life of bachelorhood. Everyone was rooting strongly for the former.

Sunny lived with her parents and six siblings at Heavenly Acres Mobile Home Park. Now in her late twenties, she had weathered a disastrous six-week marriage to a truck driver from Barre when she was a lass of seventeen, just barely dropped out of high school. Economically her life revolved around free money—welfare checks and food stamps. She did not mind hard work, but failed to see the point in doing it for someone else when the government would pay you not to.

Despite her less-than-perfect life, she retained a great half-moon smile in the middle of her square head and a booming laugh that filled a space instantly, backing all other sounds into corners. When Sue Townshend offered her a tray of marinated, stuffed grape leaves, Sunny demurred, saying:

"No thanks, vegetables make me poot like a chain saw with a clogged air intake." The subject might have been left at this point, but not with Sunny. She treated Sue to a colorful discourse on her gastrointestinal system, what foods made her fart rather than belch, the effect of cheese on her stools, and the time that she ate so many beets that when she peed she thought her period had come early.

"She's a little rough on the edges," said Emil with a grin, but Darwin told him not to worry, while Joe simply shook his hand.

The changing of years was feted without television, a descending ball in Times Square, Guy Lombardo, or digital watches. "Do you think it's time?" Darwin asked Hannah

Duncan. She nodded. They went over to her schoolhouse and rang the bell, heralding a new year to the silent trees surrounding the village. The party dissipated immediately: satisfied people returning to the sanctity of their own homes, unconcerned that it was officially still one hour before the midnight they'd already celebrated.

"Nice party," said Darwin as he and Sammi came toward the end of their cleanup. She agreed. He then kissed her lightly and went out to the sauna to begin his month of purification.

Darwin's month of asceticism was one of the most bitterly cold in the history of Vermont. When he awoke in the darkness before dawn, his first act was to rekindle the sauna stove which had to be maintained at full-tilt boogie merely to stave off the worst of the cold. Then he put on a pot filled with snow. While the water heated, Darwin stretched and exercised on a straw mat.

And he shaved. This was a concession. Darwin reasoned that his quest for purity was not aided by his patients facing a stubble bum. He could not see that slathering his face with Gillette Foamy then lopping it off with his Trac II was consistent with the plan, so he settled for warm water, a straight razor, a splash of snow, and a few drops of lime juice as an astringent. As much as anything, Darwin felt that this ritual, especially the bleeding, built his character.

Breakfast was unpolished brown rice, as was lunch and dinner, washed down with "tea" of melted snow. The only food Darwin allowed himself besides rice and water was lime juice. There was little scientific or spiritual logic to Darwin's diet. He associated brown rice with Oriental mysticism. The lime was to prevent scurvy. After a while he began drying the rinds on the stove, then throwing them in his warm-water tea. The resulting beverage was vaguely satisfying, although Darwin developed vivid fantasies about gin and tonics, an affliction that plagued him throughout the month.

By seven A.M. his mind and body were prepared for the workday. He joined the family to help with the morning ritual of browbeating the kids into meeting the school bus. Darwin tried extra hard to be helpful and cheerful. The kids appeared unaffected by his efforts to attain purity. There was noticeable coolness from Sammi, something Darwin hoped would disappear at the end of the month. Occasionally the smell of sizzling bacon or steamy coffee tested his will, but Darwin held fast. He became pure.

At work he attended to his normal routine, but without the coffee or doughnuts that he particularly favored. At noon he adjourned to Body Beautiful, the local health club where Sammi took her Jazz-ercize classes, and he pumped iron, swam, and toned his body.

Upon arriving home he set straight about doing whatever winter household chores were necessary—hauling wood, shoveling snow—then sat through dinner with the family. Once the kids were in bed, he retreated to the sauna for an evening of brown rice, lime juice, solitude, and darkness. Periodically Gimp Fenvessey stopped in, usually with a six-pack of beer, to test Darwin's resolve and to update him on the political happenings in Montpelier. Weinstein had now officially declared her candidacy and was forming her campaign organization. The governor had already indicated her enthusiasm and support. Dunwoody, meanwhile, now held the chairmanship of the Senate Appropriations Committee, his gnarly fingers securely holding the state's purse strings.

Two weeks into the venture Darwin noticed the first desirable effects. The signs were barely perceptible, yet unmistakable. Brown rice was taking on overtones of complexity, so that he no longer craved Scampi Dijon to accompany it. Lime juice proved a versatile libation that fully satisfied both his thirst as well as a need for variety. His body felt terrific; he was rounding into the best shape of his life. At work and with the children he felt clear-headed and serene, unruffled by whatever challenges or exigencies were presented him. His senses were heightened to changes in the weather. He could perceive a cloud cover from inside his sauna in the middle of the night. He could feel snowflakes on the roof. Keeping warm brought immense satisfaction, as did the identical bowel movement that he had at the same time each morning.

In the final week of the month a high-pressure system moved in, each night putting Upper Granville directly in touch with light shafts from celestial bodies. Temperatures plunged to minus thirty. Darwin had to wake every other hour to add more fuel to the fire. Cars could not start, but Darwin felt more confident than ever in his ability to survive.

On the morning of February first Darwin eschewed his warm water and brown rice. He went into the house, where the family was still asleep. He turned on the tap and reveled in the warm water. He slathered Foamy on his face and delightedly whacked it away with his Trac II, even treating himself to a new blade. Then he hopped into the shower for an langourous twenty-minute scrubbing that left no fold or crinkle of his body uncleansed.

When the family awoke, it was to a clean and jubilant father, as well as scrambled eggs, English muffins, bacon, and fresh-squeezed orange juice. The kids ate, then waddled off to the bus stop. As Sammi put dishes in the dishwasher, Darwin lolled at the table with a second cup of coffee, barely able to restrain his contentment.

"It's over," he said, his voice equal parts relief and regret. "But now I'm home, and I'm stronger than ever. I can't tell you how much I needed this month, or what it's meant to me, or how grateful I am to you for seeing me through it."

"It's over," she echoed, but without matching emotions. Her gaze was out the window to a point a million miles away. "You may be home, but I'm gone. This month has given me time to think things over too. I'm leaving you, Darwin. I've taken a small apartment in Montpelier and a volunteer job on Natalie Weinstein's campaign staff. I don't know what the future holds for us, Darwin, but I doubt I will ever come back."

Darwin regrouped and pondered fully for several minutes before responding: "Honey, I realize that the last couple of decades have been hard on you girls—"

"I'm not a 'girl'!"

"Let me finish, okay? It sounds a little stiff to say that 'the last couple of decades have been hard on the female of the species.' Anyway, you gotta raise kids, do a Ten-K in under forty minutes, cook like Paul Prudhomme, support the right causes, and combine the business savvy of Iacocca with the body of Madonna."

"What are you saying?" She did not soften, even to Darwin's pleading tone.

"That this isn't your fault, but it's not my fault, either. We're all spoiled and want everything."

"I want a multigamous relationship."

"Mull-tig-a-muss? Which magazine did that come from? And what does it mean?"

"A multigamous relationship is totally nonaccountable. I'm not saying I don't love you, Darwin, only that I am capable of loving others as well, and I want to explore those relationships."

"I thought that being accountable is what marriage is all about."

"That's not my interpretation of our agreement."

"So what relationships do you want to explore, with Georgio?"

"*Gregorio*! Maybe. And with Natalie Weinstein. And with anyone else who doesn't look on me as a meal cooker, nose blower, child transporter. I'm going to find out if there is more to life than living in Upper Granville, Vermont, with Darwin Hunter."

7

Total Disclosure

It was the most gruesome of Februarys. The ground hog came out of his hole and saw a world awash, an icy swampland, gray soup. Snowbanks wattled, pelted by a driving rain from the south, a rain so acid you could feel it through your skin. Cancerous hydrocarbons from belching smokestacks rode the upper air currents to the pristine north, where they fell as a plague on tiny hamlets.

The roads succumbed to the false signal and thawed. Then, just as abruptly as the warm rain appeared, winter reared back, a wife wronged, and slapped with all her might. The humans were at the mercy of the elements. Their mechanical inventions, studded snow tires and four-wheel drive, were useless in the frozen slush. They couldn't ski, they couldn't ignore, they could only complain.

Sammi left on a Saturday. Darwin borrowed Joe Pisano's van and helped her move into an antiseptic studio apartment, conveniently located within walking distance of the State House in Montpelier. Darwin cried. He cried a lot during the week. Sammi cried, too, but could not be moved to change her mind. The separation, by her definition, was mutual and indefinite. She needed time and space. She intended to devote herself fully to the law courses she was auditing, her various causes, the campaign of Natalie Weinstein, and the future of the Hunter family.

She never asked that he drop out of the race, and he never volunteered. The closest they came to the subject was when he asked, "If I dropped out, would it make a difference in your leaving?" To which she replied, "No."

The children, they both agreed, were better off at home. In a fortuitous turn of events for Darwin—actually, it was Sammi's inspiration—Sunny Moss agreed to live in at the Hunters', providing a range of services to lighten the domestic load.

She moved in on Monday, making the Sunday between Sammi's departure and Sunny's arrival the longest day in the family's collective existence. Darwin tried to be cheerful, but even Allison, the youngest, could see through the upbeat veneer. The weather was crummy, holding them captive. Darwin burned the grilled-cheese sandwiches, then tried to cover up by pretending it had been done on purpose. "Indian brown" was the phrase he generated to describe his cooking technique. "These aren't Indian brown," said Allison, "they're burnt."

There was nothing on television, so he took everyone into town to let them pick out a video cassette. After a full half hour of squabbling, during which consensus was not achieved, they left the store, cassetteless. I wonder, thought Darwin as he lay alone in his bed, if anyone has ever died of terminal bicker? The future looked bleak indeed.

Sunny's appearance improved their lot. She reveled in

the luxury of the home, compared to her doublewide. All this, plus she was free to spend evenings with Emil. She brought with her an indomitably positive outlook, as well as a blank slate concerning the domestic differences between Darwin and Sammi. This was the ultimate au pair, Upper Granville style, or more accurately, as Darwin described her to Joe, the ultimate au cube.

The neighbors learned of the Hunters' split either directly or indirectly. They were polite and sympathetic. Teresa Blanchard said, "I told you so"; Sue Townshend, "It serves you right." Townshend said "I can't believe it," and Tina Pisano was "shocked." Joe just shook his head slowly in his worldwise, Italian way. Stella Blanchard said, "I'm sorry"; Hoyt, "She'll come back." Walt and Martha Gunion looked the other way; Howard "Warren" Pease quoted divorce statistics. Gimp offered him a beer.

Sunny helped, with her boisterous, good-hearted treatment of the kids and her explicit explanations of every possible bodily function that involved oozing or secretion. For several weeks Darwin lay groggy on the canvas; gradually, however, he felt the return of his strength. At first it was for fleeting moments, but soon entire days during which he felt like himself. Without his month of monastic preparation, he might have slipped beneath the waves of life.

On the last Sunday of the month Darwin ate a big breakfast, then worked off most of it cross-country skiing. Later he took the kids sledding and tubing on the same hillside where Bennett Blanchard had removed Townshend Clarke's property stake. The Clarke and Pisano kids joined in; then, after everyone was completely soaked, they went into the Hunter kitchen, where Sunny cooked up a pot of hot chocolate and popcorn. As the kids were making a mess and Sunny cleaning it up, Darwin paused for a moment to sit at his desk, and woke up an hour later. That night Sunny settled in front of the television to watch a made-for-TV movie about yet another young woman with a terminal disease. Darwin suggested she invite Emil to join her. If she did not object, he would head up to the Club 100 to catch Captain Goo-Roo's Sunday-night show.

Sunny thought it was a great plan.

Gimp Fenvessey, thirty-two-years old, single, with a reasonably roguish appeal that transcended his deformity, brought to the Granville *Clarion* a piercing journalistic perspective which was wasted on most of the local populace.

Gimp lived in the Cowdrey place, a simple cape near the center of town owned by Walt Gunion. The house had been occupied by a series of northern vagabonds who strutted and fretted their hour upon the Upper Granville stage and then were heard from no more. The keeper of local statistics, Howard "Warren" Pease, could tell you that the longevity record for Cowdrey House tenants was eighteen months. The most consecutive months that Walt had collected rent was five.

Gimp differed from the average transient in that he was a bona-fide Vermonter. Reared right in Granville, Gimp's experiences from the State House to the firehouse made him a keen observer of sociopolitical and econocultural aspects of rural life. Although the son of a farmer, Gimp was not a Chuck, having sacrificed his pedigree for four years at Haverford College and then nailed the coffin with an additional year at Columbia School of Journalism.

It was the last day of the gruesome month when Gimp banged on the Hunters' door. Darwin was cleaning up dishes after a passable dinner of tortiere à la Sunny and salad à la yup. He yelled for Gimp to come in.

"Hey, Darwin. Can I borrow your torch? Mine's out of gas, and I've got a frozen pipe."

"I'm shocked. A Vermonter running out of gas during the winter? I thought only Flatlanders lacked the basic survival skills."

"Must be the Chuck in me. You've got it mixed up. One of the ways you can tell a Flatlander is that he's got his wood put up for the winter, he knows where his jumper cables are, and his chain saw will actually start on the first pull. A real native is more casual about these things. That's why we drive rear-wheel-drive cars and never get stuck, and wear sneakers all through the winter."

And it was true. Gimp was wearing tattered Reeboks.

"But still," countered Darwin, clearly relishing an intellectual challenge after a dinner of childish mayhem and Sunny's verbal account on the seven-headed boil on her father's butt that she had once lanced, "You are here, dependent on me, a Flatlander, for the necessary tool to thaw your pipes."

"Dependent, hell," protested a mock-indignant Fenvessey, "I'm duping you. You don't think it's my gas I ran out of, it's Pisano's. I borrowed his torch last week. No Vermonter would loan me a torch. If you don't believe me, try to borrow something from Hoyt Blanchard. 'Only fools loan tools,' he'd say. And he's right, fools and Flatlanders. But if you won't help me, I suppose I can go over to Hannah's, call Walt, and tell him to fix the pipes or I won't pay the rent. That's what I do whenever I'm short for the month. By the way, haven't you forgotten to offer me a beer?"

"How rude of me. Help yourself. Do you want any tortiere? Sunny made a ton."

"Tortiere!! Sacrebleu! My favorite. See what I mean about the cunning native intelligence? Next, you'll be offering to unfreeze my pipes."

"Want some help?"

"Sure, I could use an extra hand."

It took Gimp and Darwin more than three hours to locate the freeze-ups and to apply enough heat to liberate the taps. The work was tedious but very easy, the bulk of the time passed in quiet conversation while the blowtorch hissed its flame onto the culprit pipes. Darwin and Gimp felt comfortable in the fieldstone womb. Darwin shared the thoughts and feelings of his month of bachelorhood, while Gimp regaled him with more insights into the scurrilous nature of Linwood "Woody" Dunwoody.

"So you're really going ahead with your campaign?"

"Yup," answered Darwin. "I will be formally announcing sometime in the next month."

"Hey," said Gimp, visibly excited by the generation of an idea, "why don't you make your announcement at the Fools Fling?"

"I guess because I don't know what the Fools Fling is."

"You invented the Fools Fling," insisted Fenvessey.

"What are you talking about?"

Fenvessey was skeptical. "Walt and Townshend haven't talked to you about the Fools Fling?" Darwin shook his head. Gimp was so disbelieving that he had to ask the question again: "They haven't said a single word to you about the Fools Fling?"

"No."

"You're not shitting me, Darwin?"

"No."

"Then sit down."

Darwin sat on the third tier of the cellar steps. Gimp rushed upstairs and returned within thirty seconds. He brought back fresh beers for both of them, as well as a large envelope bearing the letterhead of a New York public relations firm and the large stamped message: FOR IMMEDIATE RELEASE. Darwin removed the contents, a packet of printed sheets and eight-by-ten black-and-white glossies.

Darwin heard Fenvessey say, "More than five thousand of these went out to newspapers, radio and television stations, yesterday. I got mine in the mail today."

Darwin read aloud the headline on the top piece: "Traditional Festival Provides Colorful Backdrop for Historical Development Ground Breaking."

For the next fifteen minutes Darwin pored over the press releases, backgrounders, photos, and captions describing the elaborate plans of two aggressive yet adamantly preservationist developers to make a reality of 1839. The official ground-breaking was scheduled for April first—April Fool's Day—and according to the release, an annual day of celebrating the rites of spring in the Northland.

"I can't believe it," moaned Darwin every thirty seconds or so.

Gimp continued to diddle with the torch, and returned, "I can't believe you didn't know about this!"

Occasionally, the moans were replaced by Darwin's blurts of disbelief: "It says I revived the tradition! . . . It's taking place at my house! . . . They're giving away copies of *Beyond Yonder*! . . . It calls me a rural pundit! . . . It says that more than five hundred units are planned . . . It says negotiations are nearly complete . . . It says you're the local press liaison!"

Gimp shrugged. "In return for free rent, Walt can call me most anything he wants."

Just then a gurgling noise signaled the return of movement to the water. "Hey," said Gimp, "mission accomplished. Here, shake my flipper."

He offered the deformed limb to Darwin, who was still seated on the step, overwhelmed with the contents of the press release. There was momentary hesitation, which Gimp dispelled quickly by saying, "Believe me, Darwin, I had no idea this was done without your knowledge." Darwin smiled, believed him, grabbed the nub and shook.

He smiled. "There must be some way to turn this into opportunity."

Darwin was fully prepared the next evening when he came home and saw Townshend's Lincoln Town Car waiting in the driveway. The indignation had passed, as had the need for vengeance and the desire to gum up the works out of pure spite. Darwin had met his campaign manager, Billy Mann, for breakfast, and together they had devised a plan to make the Fools Fling work to their advantage.

"Hi, Walt. Hey, Townie. What's up?" he said brightly.

Oh, nothing much, they said noncommittally, just want to bounce a few ideas off you. Great, said Darwin, why don't you wait in my study. I need to say hi to the kids and check in with Sunny.

He made them wait for a half an hour, while he played with the kids, read the mail, had a beer and watched the weather report on television. Almost to sap season. When he joined Walt and Townshend, he was the image of friendliness, although he pointedly did not offer them a libation.

"It was a few months ago," began Townshend, obviously rehearsed, "that we shared with you our plans for 1839. We've made terrific progress since then, and we wanted to fill you in. I think I can summarize by saying that Upper Granville is on the brink of the most exciting period in its entire history."

"And you're a big part of it," interjected Walt.

Darwin sat in his desk chair and listened to his virtues extolled, how the strength of his personality had galvanized a community, helping to revive cultural traditions then recording them for posterity in his book—Walt called it "a rural masterpiece"—*Beyond Yonder*. He nodded politely and demurred modestly, keeping in check the tongue that could lash and shackle this duo faster than one could say "hypocrite."

Townshend presented the status of 1839 as being consistent with the program presented several months earlier, but on a less ambitious timetable.

"We still want to end up in the same place," he said, using his hands in a way that he must have learned from a self-help video, "but we realize that the local populace is going to take longer than we had anticipated to embrace the vision we have of the community. That's why we have not pressed the issue with the Darwin Hunters and Bennett Blanchards of the world."

"Because we need your help," said Walt submissively.

"And because we're friends and neighbors," chimed in Townshend.

"And because when Bennett sees how we handle things, he'll start getting serious about negotiations."

Darwin chuckled and said simply: "Go on."

To hear Townshend present it, he and Walt just had this idea and they wanted Darwin's input. Everyone had such a good time at the horseshoe match that Darwin had organized two years ago, a revival of a vernal festival called the Spring Fling, that they thought they should do it again. Perhaps they could make it a little bigger and better than last time. Yeah, maybe get a tent in case it snowed.

Yeah, or maybe three tents in case it snows a lot, added Darwin. Townshend and Walt snuck a look at each other. Their press release had mentioned three tents. Coincidence, they decided. Just Darwin being his usual hyperbolic self.

And we'll revive the horseshoe match, and what about this? We'll all dress in costume like we did at your New Year's party, Darwin.

Great! And Stella will bake a pie. And I'll play my guitar. We could even do a pig roast.

Er, sure, Darwin. In fact, let's have a band. You know, contra-dance band, traditional stuff.

Whoa, said Darwin. Now you're talking big bucks. I'm willing to contribute, but let's not go crazy.

"Tell you what," said Townshend, picking up on Darwin's perfect lead. "Why don't we have our company sponsor the whole thing? Then it won't cost anyone anything. We'll just write off the whole Fools Fling."

"I thought it was the Spring Fling?" needled Darwin.

" 'Fools Fling' has a catchier ring, don't you think, Darwin?" said Walt, his brow furrowing with the potential glitch.

"How can you justify the write-off?" asked Darwin.

"Oh," said Townshend nonchalantly, as if he had been doing these things all of his life, "we'll do something quasi-official. Maybe call it the official ground breaking for 1839. We'll have Gimp there to do a little piece for the local paper. Just something to make it legit."

"I see, I see. I've never been involved with these things before." Darwin put on his most innocent face.

"Darwin," said Walt, his timing, as usual, superb, "do you mind if we use your place for the event? It's the appropriate place, right here in the middle of town."

"No problem," said Darwin. The other men could not resist an exchange of smiles to punctuate their successful close. Darwin rambled on, "We can get together in a couple of weeks to dig out the old horseshoe court. That'll be a good way to get some exercise on a Saturday."

"That won't be necessary," said Townshend, already rising and reaching for his coat, satisfied at having bagged his unsuspecting prey. "We want you to know that you won't have to lift a finger for this event. It won't cost you a penny."

"You won't even have people wanting to use your bathroom."

"Why not, Walt?" Townshend immediately noticed his partner's misstep and changed the subject:

"Say, Darwin, we'd like to get a few copies of your book. Should we get them through you or directly from the printer?"

"The printer," answered Darwin.

"Good," said Townshend, "so we're all set. The Fools Fling will be held here on April first." He held out his hand.

Darwin reached out, stopping mere inches short of Townshend's hand. "Hey," he said brightly, "how about I officially announce my candidacy for State Senate at the same time?"

Townshend's face clouded and there was an ominous second of silence. "I don't know that the occasion would be appropriate for anything quite so serious."

"Me, serious? A plague on you. Don't you see? A lot of people think of me as a fool, so what could be more appropriate than to kick off the campaign at the Fools Fling?"

"Okay, Darwin, I suppose you could make a brief and simple announcement."

"We'd hate to make this thing too political," added Walt.

"Right," said Darwin. "Just like we don't want to make it too commercial. Don't worry," he grabbed Townshend's hand, then Walt's, "I'll just make, you know, a simple announcement."

The crews started work on the Hunter festival site the next week, first plowing free the field next to the house, then bringing in tents, porta-potties, podiums, staging, portable heaters, power, and seating for half the populace of Central Vermont. Walt and Townshend were on the sight full time, and although the understatement of their plan was now obvious, Darwin did not press the issue.

"He's too intimidated to say anything," chortled Walt.

Of the three tents, one was for logistical support, one for exclusive press use, one for the Fools Fling activities. By now the plans were public, the release having been picked up statewide. Gimp Fenvessey told Darwin that the budget for the entire affair was just over a hundred thousand dollars, much of which was being spent to fly in journalists and film crews from New York.

"This is a major-league operation," said Gimp.

"Masterminded by a couple of bush leaguers," said Darwin, completing the thought.

The locals agreed. Curious area residents began cruising the valley just as they did in the days preceding deer season. Central Vermont had never seen the likes of this.

Fenvessey ticked off the attending dignitaries. *Time* was

sending a staffer; CBS, NBC, and ABC had arranged for local affiliates to attend. *Colonial Homes* was planning a cover story. Charles Kuralt was rumored to be on his way. The list went on.

The roster of speakers was equally impressive. The governor would be there, sandwiched between an environmental expert and a historian paid to sing the praises of 1839. A museum curator, president of the American Preservation Society, and Riley Gore were also on the roster. So was Linwood "Woody" Dunwoody, as the incumbent state senator. A minor flap developed when Natalie Weinstein and the other declared candidate, Mimi Cox, protested that they, too, should be allowed to speak. "Tough cookies," came the response from Walt and Townshend, who had already relegated Darwin to the final speaker's position, figuring that the bulk of the crowd would leave by that time. They agreed to let Weinstein and Cox attend, however, and to distribute leaflets from small tables in the back.

Programs were printed with full details three days before the event. The title of Darwin's address was "Total Disclosure." Gimp Fenvessey stopped by to drop off a program at the Hunter household.

"I saw Sammi down here today," said the reporter.

"So I heard. A little tough on her, I imagine, having to beg for a speaking slot for an event held at her own home," returned Darwin.

"She didn't look too happy."

"I can imagine. So what do you make of this whole deal?"

Gimp laughed. "It's a circus, but a bunch of my pals from J school are using it as an excuse to come north. It's going to be a two-day party that someone else is footing the bill for. A lot of media people are using it to catch a last ski weekend, so attendance will be good even though there is not a helluva lot of newsworthiness to this 1839 business. Some reporters are taking the angle of showing how this event is a shameless manipulation of the press. Tell me, what is 'Total Disclosure' all about?"

Darwin hesitated. He liked Gimp, but reminded himself that Gimp was a reporter. But he was also a neighbor whose pipes would likely need thawing again. Darwin balanced the loyalties, then told him everything, taking time to answer Gimp's inquiries along the way. He finished with the Hunter signature, the wiseass rhetorical question:

"So whaddya think? Can you convince any of your J school buddies to stay through my speech?"

Fenvessey let out a long, low breath before replying: "Darwin, Total Disclosure is an idea whose time has come. If my nose for news is right, you'll be giving a lot of people the justification they need for this junket. I'll be there with bells on, and as many others as I can possibly convince. Who knows? In a few days you might be a household word."

Journalists, dignitaries, and curiosity seekers began arriving on Thursday afternoon for the Friday circus. Townshend and Walt were models of hysteria, flanked by "agency guys," advisors, and architects. They were on top of every new arrival, flashing plans and offering favors. Meanwhile, Darwin prepared for his pig roast inside the logistics tents. Captain Goo-Roo arrived and set up a makeshift stage. Darwin commandeered a keg. They were ready.

Darwin lit the fire just as darkness fell. The temperature

plummeted and the relative softness of the sunny day returned to the harshness of winter. There was a sumptuous buffet in the press tent, but little else aside from the roar of the propane heaters. Walt and Townshend had not planned entertainment for the evening. The out-of-towners faced a bleak evening at the local hostelries where they were housed, so were easily attracted to the music emanating from the logistics tent.

Most had never seen a pig roast and were fascinated by Darwin's skilled trussing of the beast to the huge spit. With little else to do, in an isolated environment conducive to the establishment of new friendships, they were quick to offer help turning the spit and tending the fire. Gimp's friends formed a lively nucleus, and the group grew as quickly as a snowball rolling downhill.

Captain Goo-Roo was at his maniacal best, playing guitar, mandolin, banjo, electric piano, Jew's harp, mouth harp, trombone, French horn, car horn, beer keg, anything that would make a sound. He played mostly requests, with zany segues into related themes, musical and otherwise. He was also a human commercial for Darwin's upcoming speech:

"Let's start the countdown, all you groovy sophisticates. Only eighteen hours until Darwin Hunter's 'Total Disclosure.' You will find out why this may be the only honest man left in America. You may think I'm exaggerating, but this is the biggest speech in America since the Gettysburg Address. You'll tell your grandchildren about this."

"I'll tell my grandchildren about this, but it won't be because of 'Total Disclosure.' " The speaker was a feature writer for the Home section of the *New York Times*. The Captain always knew that he was working the crowd successfully when he could get people to talk to him. This crowd was isolated, disoriented, full of anticipation, and in the palm of Captain Goo-Roo's strong hand.

"Then on with the countdown. This song is named after a satellite. I play the organ part on my kazoo. If you've got any rhythm, I've got a tambourine, maracas, and a big cardboard box that, if you've had enough beers, sounds like a bass drum. So come on and help me and we'll count down to 'Total Disclosure' with an original from Johnny and the Hurricanes called 'Telstar.' "

The beer flowed, the pig sizzled, and the One Mann Jam had a collection of world-weary journalists clapping, banging, hooting, whistling, and finding rhythm deep within their souls. Darwin wore his apron and rotated volunteers to turn the spit. Like Tom Sawyer painting his fence, there was barely enough work to go around. Occasionally he would poke a tumescent pocket and a stream of grease would roar into flame, bringing cheers from all the revelers. Inspired, he ran into the house and dragged out Sunny to lance a few. She loved it, and entertained her own claque of free-lance wire-service photographers until the wee hours.

By eleven o'clock the logistics tent was as filled with warmth and humanity as an Irish pub on Saturday night. Gimp's J school buddies broke into another keg and some rolls intended for the next day's luncheon. Darwin began whacking off outer hunks of pork that were done, and Sunny served them up to the patrons whose taste buds had been titillated all night long. A blond lady, who claimed to do a food column for *Yankee*, wiped the juice from her chin and proclaimed this the best example of simple American fare she had ever tasted. Captain Goo-Roo, meanwhile, had the group yipping and shoo-bopping, each song finishing to cheers, hoots, and more requests.

The journalists were eventually shuttled back to their inns and motels for the night. The only late partyers were Gimp's friends, who took over the keg and spit duties from Darwin at midnight. "Don't forget to get some sleep," Darwin called back to them.

"Don't worry," they assured him. "We'll be there for 'Total Disclosure.' "

Darwin Hunter rose as his name was called and walked to the podium. He nodded to Billy Mann, Captain Goo-Roo, who awaited him at the microphone. Billy had just completed the first public performance of "Total Disclosure," a hard-rocking ballad with a central theme of disillusionment built around a rousing chorus fraught with social significance. The song described politicians, parents, and community leaders who had in common only the fact that they were not what they seemed. The crowd joined in enthusiastically each time the chorus came, a testament to the dullness of what had preceded Billy Mann, more than anything else.

The applause now died to a smatter. Darwin cleared his voice, mostly to hear what it sounded like through the microphone. He began:

"My name is Darwin Hunter."

In the back he could see Sammi seated at the small table she shared with Natalie Weinstein. There was a sea of faces, perhaps a total of two hundred fifty. Sunny stood at the back of the tent with Emil and the Blanchard clan. Bennett and Teresa had aroused the only real excitement of the day, by picketing the entrance to the tent with placards saying Leave Us Alone! Now, however, their point made, their curiosity had gotten the better of them, so they were taking in the show along with everyone else.

"And I would like to lead the residents of the Fifth District of the state of Vermont."

The day had gone well enough from Walt's and Townshend's perspective. The weather cooperated, giving them a brilliant if breezy day. The turnout for the morning events was very light, too many of the journalists having opted to sleep in after spending the evening in the logistics tent. By lunchtime, however, the crowd showed signs of life. Overall there had been enough note taking, camera clicking, and on-camera interviews to convince them that the event was a success. Walt and Townshend had expected the climactic event to be their press conference right after lunch. They were surprised when no one left when they turned the stage over to Darwin and his kooky musician friend.

"In considering the worthiness of my candidacy I have done a great deal of thinking. I have thought about our society, the human species, and the written and unwritten laws that govern us all. What I have concluded is that there is something that counts more than education, more than experience, and more than patriotism. I'm talking about honesty."

The mood of the crowd was mixed. Many of the people who had met Darwin over the roasting pig the night before were expecting something comical. Their curiosity was piqued, but they anticipated nothing of consequence from the political candidacy of a nobody from nowhere. Darwin's friends and neighbors were a little more on edge. They had known Darwin long enough to know that he made rules rather than followed them.

"I have no experience. I'm a doctor, an eye doctor, not a great one, but good enough. But I am honest. At least I will be by the end of today. So many of our leaders have disappointed us in recent years. They get us to believe in them, then we find out they are completely false. Richard Nixon, Jim Jones, Jim and Tammy Faye Bakker, Gary Hart—the list of deceivers is as long as the list of leaders."

The crowd was politely quiet. Curiosity has that effect on a crowd.

"I am not going to tell you that I am a moral paragon, because I am not a moral paragon. But I won't disillusion you. My policy is one of Total Disclosure. If I am to lead, my constituents have a right to know who is leading them. When I was eight years old I stole. I stole the milk money that my mother gave me and used it to buy baseball cards and candy. When she caught me, I promised never to steal again. I lied. When I was thirteen I stole a forty-five record from a Woolworth's. The record was "Walking with My Angel" by Bobby Vee. I never liked the record after that. Later that year I stole a copy of *Playboy* that I kept in the arm of my fishing jacket until my mother found it."

Thus began a forty-minute journey into the seamy underside of Darwin Hunter's life. He told of masturbating in a movie theater, lying about his age to buy liquor, killing a sparrow with a BB gun, and sending a teacher an anonymous note turning in a fellow classmate known to be cheating on tests.

The saga continued through high school into college, where Darwin admitted to a multitude of peccadillos, including smoking dope and lurid, though infrequent sex. On and on he went, meeting Sammi, revealing the most intimate details of their relationship up through and including bouts of impotency and the precarious state of their current relationship.

The portrait did not dwell exclusively on the negative. He brought forth in a straightforward manner that he was a bright, diligent guy who had succeeded in many of life's endeavors due to a willingness to put forth more effort than the next guy. Darwin thought he had conducted himself with an overall sense of decency and consistency that showed the type of man he was.

But, oh the wounds. They were not pretty. There were four traffic tickets; the time he was grounded by his college dean for keeping a girl in his room overnight; the night at the opthalmologists' convention when he passed out in the room of a female doctor; the time his own wife tried to have him arrested for drunk driving; the time he chipped his son's tooth by playing too roughly; Sammi's critique of him as a chauvinist, weakling, and a coward, not to mention the fact that she was working for his opponent.

Darwin paused and tried to read the crowd before entering into his close. They were rapt. Either bewildered or awed. He could not tell.

"That, in a giant nutshell, is it. I cannot disappoint you, because you know exactly what I am. You have complete access to my tax records and bank statements, because I have told you all there is to tell. My policy is, and will continue to be, one of Total Disclosure. I urge my opponents to adopt it as well. I urge people in public service everywhere to adopt Total Disclosure. In fact, anyone can benefit from Total Disclosure. We are what we are, no more, no less, and the sooner we can admit this by being honest with ourselves and others, then the sooner we will be able to put false issues of personality behind us and achieve true progress. Personally, I am now totally disclosed, and I feel great."

8

The Campaign of Bottled Beers

Darwin left the stage to a deafening murmur. As he reached the edge and descended, a hand grabbed his, gave it a warm squeeze, and he heard a woman's voice:

"You can count on my full support in your campaign."

He looked up into the blue eyes of Teresa Blanchard. The last hour had caused emotional trauma for Teresa more turbulent than the waters of Tomar Brook after a thunderstorm. Earlier, as he began his sordid confession, she had considered racing to Bennett's pickup, getting the rifle from the rear window, and shooting Darwin between the eyes before he disclosed a certain one-night stand with a local farmer's wife during a late night at the Tunbridge Fair.

But as Teresa stood transfixed, a prisoner facing the firing squad, wishing for the ground to swallow her, a miracle occurred: the speech suddenly ended. Darwin told every smarmy detail of his life, except one. She turned quickly to her mother-in-law, standing to her right, and asked for confirmation: "Did he say anything about cheating on his wife?"

"No," said Stella. "He said he was true to his wife and that he paid all his taxes. He confessed to just about everything else, though."

But Teresa was rushing the stage before Stella placed the period on her sentence. Now she spoke to Darwin with a passion and warmth that she had not shown since their night of shared lust: "Darwin, I thought you were going to blow everything, but now I see what a shrewd operator you are. Politics is lying and cheating, and you'll be able to lie and cheat better than anyone. I'm behind you all the way."

Teresa was pushed aside by others surging forward. Darwin, now acting like a seasoned politician, instinctively sought out the gaze of his campaign manager, Billy Mann, for an instant review. How'd I do? asked Darwin with a look. The Captain gave him the thumbs up.

The opinion of the crowd, however, was sharply divided, and this became apparent in the many press reports over the next few weeks. Gimp Fenvessey was right. Within a week Total Disclosure was part of the American lexicon, and for several days Darwin Hunter was a household word.

Sammi Hunter described Darwin's Total Disclosure to Dan Rather as "the most humiliating experience of my life. He feels unburdened, and I feel stripped naked on national TV." She made this assessment despite Darwin's public professions of love and entreaties for her to return home. Natalie Weinstein, quoted in the *New York Times*, called Total Disclosure "political hara-kiri." Asked whether or not she might totally disclose, she replied, "Get serious."

Mimi Cox, the banker's virtuous wife, described Darwin

in *Ms.* as a "sick puppy," suggesting professional care as a possible remedy. Linwood "Woody" Dunwoody told *Newsweek* that Total Disclosure was "a desperate, purely political maneuver by a little man on a dead horse." The voters of Central Vermont, according to Dunwoody, would laugh Hunter off the ballot.

The neighbors were divided. Stella thought the speech "courageous," although she wished he had left out the parts about "playing with himself." Hannah Duncan said she respected Darwin and would consider Total Disclosure for herself. Emil Dummerston Weed could not understand the fuss. "I done lotsa stuff worsen Darwin." Hoyt Blanchard just scratched his head.

Tina Pisano said Darwin went "too far." Total Disclosure, she maintained, would have been just as effective had he omitted the graphic sexual admissions. Sue Clarke professed surprise to hear herself among the women that Darwin had known carnally in his mind, but said, "that was the only normal thing about him." Joe admired Darwin, declaring that it takes guts to disembowel yourself before the whole world. Townshend and Walt objected that Darwin had gone over his ten-minute allotment, but were too involved in their own project to realize how badly they had been upstaged.

The wire services and networks summarized the Universal implications of the story. Editorials from the Granville *Clarion* to the *Washington Post* considered the subject. Was this the last honest man? Or was this an indication of a new low ebb in the morals of society? Had Darwin Hunter single-handedly reversed the national plunge into the depths of moral turpitude? Or had smarminess become a new political tactic? For weeks the debate raged over dinner tables, in dormitory rooms, and around coffee machines. Then, as suddenly as it began, Total Disclosure became yesterday's news.

Within the Fifth District of Central Vermont, however, the flames continued to burn strong. Was this guy a nut or a saint? TOTAL DISCLOSURE bumper stickers became common; as did others exhorting Darwin to KICK BUTT. Teresa Blanchard initiated an UDDERLY HONEST sticker that found itself on the cars and tractors of the Dairymen for Darwin. To the chagrin of his opponents, Darwin's instant celebrity now made him a force to be reckoned with.

There was negative fallout as well. The Vermont Medical Association Ethic's Committee demanded an investigation to see whether Darwin should be allowed to continue to practice. A Montpelier attorney tried unsuccessfully to file sodomy charges against Darwin for his confessions of masturbation as a teenager (the statute of limitations had expired). A Burlington woman claimed he had fathered her four illegitimate children, but no one believed her, particularly when it came out that she had leveled similar charges at Barry Manilow, Robert Redford, and Pete Rose.

Darwin met nightly with Captain Goo-Roo to plan strategy. They convened in the twilight of Darwin's darkened office, at a corner table in the Club 100, or in the Hunter home over countless bottles of Genesee Bock Beer.

"Don't let it go to your head," said Billy with uncharacteristic seriousness as he studied a wire-service story on Darwin that had been printed in the San Francisco *Chronicle*. "Votes in California don't do you any good. You got lucky, but only hard work is going to convert this break into success."

Darwin's respect for Captain Goo-Roo grew steadily. Billy Mann had been the principal architect of the Total Disclosure strategy, taking Darwin's incoherent desires and turning them into a specific program. And it was his energetic pumping at the Fools Fling that turned attention from 1839 to the pending announcement. Now that the ball was rolling, he was busily nailing Darwin's feet to the floor.

Darwin waited patiently for the Captain to tell him the next move. Billy Mann's speeches were sometimes marked by prolonged silences, as if he were tuning his instrument before continuing.

"No more interviews for a while. We've got to save press coverage for when we need it. Tell anyone who calls that you will speak only to regional media until September fifteenth. Got it? That way the local guys feel good because the big dogs are asking them for news. Also, you'll get put on a few follow-up calendars for September fifteenth, when you might be able to use a shot in the arm."

"Tunbridge Fair time," said Darwin wistfully. The Tunbridge World's Fair was for Central Vermonters the last blowout of the summer season. Billy Mann continued his thoughts, as did Darwin his reverie.

"You've got to culture the groups, like that State Organization of Women (SOW) that Teresa Blanchard belongs to. And this Dairymen for Darwin thing is terrific. We'll keep pressing on the Total Disclosure theme. Dunwoody will never disclose, because he's probably indictable on a thousand counts; Weinstein is a dyke—sorry, Darwin, I shouldn't have said that—and Mimi Cox would no more publicly disclose herself than she would . . ." The Captain searched for the right image. Darwin found it:

". . . bite the head off a parakeet."

"That's right." Billy studied his friend, who was fixated on his bottle of Genesee Bock. Darwin had almost stopped drinking since his January in the sauna, but the right environment and the right brew still tapped a deep instinct. "Are you okay?"

Darwin replied, "Healthy, yes. In shape, yes. Well-fed, prosperous, able to leap tall buildings in a single bound, yes. But okay, not really."

"Was it my comment about Weinstein?"

"Not the comment so much as the prospect of the truth. My wife has lost that loving feeling."

"Reminds me of a tune."

"Yeah, right. I called Sammi and asked her out for a date. She shot me down. Bang, bang."

The Captain laughed with his lips sealed—two blasts through his nasal passages, a silent steam whistle. "Should we stop?" he said, putting a hand on Darwin's shoulder.

It was Darwin's first human touch, aside from the kids, in weeks. "No, let's go."

"Okay. For the next few weeks I want you in research. Spend every night with maps and phone books. You're going to have to cover some turf, but not now. If you contact people too far before the election, they'll forget about you. And you have to assess your competition honestly. Analyze their strengths and weaknesses. Be brutally honest." Billy Mann stopped and heh-heh-heh'd into his own beer, adding a parenthetical: "That's easy for me to say."

"Well, here's a question for you." Darwin faced him directly. "What's in this for you? A job on the road crew?"

Billy laughed. "Can you see it, with my stage moves and one of those fluorescent flags?"

"The chicks got the flags these days."

"Right. What I want, my blue-blooded friend, is for you to serve the people."

"Sounds noble."

"Don't get sarcastic on me. I want you to win and you to serve. That's it." The Captain looked deep, beyond Darwin's eyes and into his soul, then added, "And afterward I'll write a hit song about the whole experience."

It was a leisurely spring for Darwin. The trees popped the first weekend in May, and the dandelions exploded like golden flashbulbs on the green carpet of the valley floor. Life whirled around him. Darwin spent infinite hours at the backyard picnic table, poring over area topographical maps, planning where he would be every minute of every day between August first and November second, Election Day.

For the first time since moving to Vermont, Darwin considered not having a garden, devoting all his energy, instead, to the campaign. Certainly between work, the children, and the campaign, he did not have a surplus of time, nor was there any economic motivation. Reason, therefore, dictated that the garden lie fallow. Darwin watched sadly as the weeds sprouted, remembering fondly the passionate bickering between Sammi and himself about the proper techniques and placement of various seeds. Despite their many differences, eventually the rocky patch of Vermont topsoil gave nurturing life to ordered rows of plants.

"Jeezum," said Darwin, with conviction, to the greening hills. "You can't live in Vermont and not have a garden. That's why you live here in the first place."

The next day was bright and warm. Darwin threw himself into pitchforking, removing his shirt by midmorning, reveling in dirt, rocks, black flies, and manure, making up for lost time. He eschewed the aid of Joe Pisano's Roto-tiller. He needed the feeling of earth under his fingernails.

Meanwhile, the kids cast off their winter shackles and screeched in vernal delight, racing around the yard, often with Sunny in hot pursuit. She moved like a middle guard, no match for the nimble footwork of Duke, Allison, and Darwin Jr., but the chase was spirited. God forbid she ever catch one of them.

Another luxury was Bobby Pisano, Joe's fourteen-year-old, who had hired on as official mower of the lawn. The insatiable material needs of a teenager assured Darwin that Bobby would relieve him of this most thankless of summer chores. Moreover, Bennett Blanchard, Emil, and Hoyt were in seasonal frenzy, whipping back and forth on their assorted John Deeres, rearranging the organic masses of the valley.

By mid-afternoon Darwin's fingers were blistered, his back permanently bent, the venom from blackflies coursing through his veins. He would never again be clean. The garden was less than a quarter finished. He had tried to do the work of two people over several weeks in a day. He'd failed. He sat down in the loose earth, his mind awash with memories of shared labor and mulch, of the sweetness of fresh peas on the Fourth of July and the flashy brightness of sweet peas on Labor Day. No one would tell him where to plant the radishes this year; no one would limit the number of zucchinis; no one would care.

Darwin sat surrounded by spring, fresh air filled with the squeals and whirs of procreation, and never felt more alone. He cried like a baby, all the while clinging to his conviction that there must be a garden, this year and every year.

"What good is it to be king," he babbled aloud, "when there is no one to argue with about zucchini?"

* * *

As Darwin sat bawling in the garden, his political momentum was maintained by Billy Mann and Teresa Blanchard. Billy took care of the quiet work, making sure Darwin's name was on the ballot and that he produced the required petition with one hundred signatures. Teresa was infused with evangelical fervor. She mobilized farm wives to sticker their husbands' tractors. She dragged Darwin to meetings where he patiently explained to groups of staring women that he did not know the first thing about milk-support subsidies, whole-herd buyouts, or any of the issues that concerned them directly.

"Can you believe it?" interjected Teresa. "A politician who admits his ignorance? This is a man we can trust." And the ladies agreed; each unanswered question confirmed their confidence in the fact that this was one of their own.

One night Darwin sat with a map and a yellow legal pad, planning his August thrust. The phone rang but he did not stir, since Sunny regarded it as a major affront if someone other than herself answered it. After a minute she opened the back door and announced, "It's your mom."

Darwin took a quick sip of his gin and tonic, his first of the season. God, it was a million miles and four hundred light-years since he lay in the cold darkness of the sauna and craved one of these. He went inside and picked up the receiver, anxious for the voice that instantly conveyed acceptance and security:

"Hello."

"Darwin, how are you?"

"I'm very relaxed, Mom, but I'm not very happy."

"You forgot that today was Mother's Day."

"Aw. I'm sorry."

"Doesn't matter. I think the kids should do something for you."

"Maybe they could take me out to dinner at Nino's Nook. On Mother's Day they give all moms a free choice of pudding, Jell-O, or vanilla ice cream for dessert. It's quite a deal."

"That's the spirit. Do something to cheer yourself up, son."

Darwin promised that he would. Upon hanging up, he decided to investigate the noise from the front yard. The kids were excited about something. He looked out to see Emil, Sunny, and the children playing with two young piglets.

"Hey Darwin," drawled Emil, "I've got a deal you can't refuse. I'm looking for a partner in pigship."

"You're not going to keep those at your house," said Darwin, wrinkling his nose to make it obvious that his displeasure was purely olfactory.

"Naw, Walt's letting me build a pen up to his place, but I don't need two porkers. Three, if you count Sunny." He held his hands up for protection as she rained him with playful blows.

"What's the deal?"

"You pay for the piglets. They're forty bucks each. We split the cost of feed. I do all the feedin' and work. And you help me load 'em comes fall."

"Sounds fair to me."

The children cheered. Allison, however, protested that the pigs were too cute to kill and eat. Darwin assured her they would not be by fall.

"Which one you want, Darwin?"

"What's the difference?"

"Well, the sex for starters. One's a boy 'n one's a girl. And their names."

"What are their names?"

"Dunwoody and Weinstein. I'd call'em Dunny and Whiney."

"I like it," said Darwin, brightening. "And I'm done whining. Give me half of each."

9

More Straddlin'

Riley Gore had a cold, and amazingly, the world still turned. The technicians mumbled along, murmuring to each other through an electronic world of headsets and wires, the guests sat stiffly, awaiting their cues, and the host of Vermont's most popular chat show, *Straddlin the Fence*, fumed over a medical emergency table set up just out of camera view.

"I can't believe this goddamn state," said Gore, four types of lozenges clacking in his mouth. "It's goddamn July and I have a cold. And where do I catch it? At a goddamn barbecue where you can see your goddamn breath! It's goddamn July and you can see your breath!"

The technicians were unconcerned. Gore had not missed a show in nine years, although at least fifty percent of the time he had to miraculously arise from his deathbed to do so. The joke on the set was that when the Gray Fox's time finally came, three days later he would show up in time for taping.

The guests, too, ignored Gore. Natalie Weinstein, the Democratic candidate, sat closest to the host. She pored over three-by-five index cards crammed with writing in a meticulous penmanship that Darwin recognized as his wife's. Next to her sat Mimi Cox, the community stalwart and challenger to Dunwoody for the Republican standard. She was nervous, alternately clearing her throat and taking sips of water. Dunwoody was next, every wart and crinkle on his face exuding confidence, then Darwin Hunter, the independent, he of Total Disclosure, relaxed and unconcerned. At this moment his mind was back in Upper Granville, thinking of a Whiffle-ball game he'd played that afternoon with the kids.

This is the second meeting of the month for the candidates. Each marched in the Granville Fourth of July parade, their presentations reflections of their campaigns. Cox rode the float for the Christian Summer Bible School. Weinstein marched solo, nattily dressed in a double-breasted gray suit, accompanying each of her brochures with a firm handshake and no-nonsense smile. Dunwoody rode majestically on a handsome Morgan horse, a team of minions distributing literature and handing candy to children while the senator smiled, waved, and shot a six gun into the air whenever he sensed the crowd's attention wandering.

Darwin's display was the grandest of all. Aided by his nine-year-old son, Darwin recruited twelve fourth graders to form the BMX Brigade, a precision driving team of stunt drivers. There was crowd-pleasing music, of course, in the form of Captain Goo-Roo, the One Mann Jam, and the antics of the candidate himself, who led the crowd in providing musical accompaniment.

"Thirty seconds," said a technician.

"Goddamn state," said Gore, spitting his lozenges into a plastic cup and spraying his gaping yaw with an atomizer before transforming into the lovable Gray Fox.

"Good luck," said Mimi Cox to Natalie Weinstein, who responded with a laser-beam stare that burned holes in her opponent's head. Cox turned to Dunwoody to try her fortunes. "Good luck," she chirped.

"Fuck you," mouthed Dunwoody, inaudibly yet unmistakably. Cox smiled and nodded pleasantly, as if the man had just complimented her on her dress. The blood in her head, however, drained rapidly. Dunwoody sneaked a wink at Darwin, who had observed the exchange.

"A little lesson in hard ball," he smirked conspiratorially. Darwin, who had been thinking Whiffle ball, realized that Dunwoody expected him to share vicariously in the brutal put-down.

"Ten seconds," came the call. Gore did his eyebrow flick, asked Weinstein how he looked, then froze his smile for the camera before she could reply:

"Well, howdy-hi, and welcome to another edition of *Straddlin' the Fence*, Vermont's show of what's new and what's, well, just plain interesting. I'm your host, Riley Gore, the Gray Fox of the Green Mountains, and tonight we have a special political show with four candidates for the Senate seat in the Fifth District. They are Natalie Weinstein, Vermont Law School professor and a familiar figure in many activist groups. Mimi Cox, an alto in the Evangeline Church Choir and chairman—or I guess I should say chairmistress—of SANITY, which, as we all know, stands for Say 'Absolutely Not' in Teenage Years. To her right is Linwood 'Woody' Dunwoody, a prominent, some would say 'legendary' fixture on the state political scene. And finally Darwin Hunter, a dark horse candidate—"

"Some would say 'dead horse!' " blurted Dunwoody, who then led the candidates and Gore in a booming chorus of laughter.

"I know a story about a dead horse," said Gore, addressing Dunwoody directly. He then babbled on about the one-legged postman in Sussex Junction who caused some neophyte Flatlanders to flee Vermont in screaming terror when he sent them to a picnic site next to the town rendering plant. It was not a very funny story, but Dunwoody guffawed so frequently that Gore could barely deliver the punchline: the rendering plant foreman horrified the Flatlanders by releasing gas from the stomach of a bloated beast with one swift stroke of an ax. The others simply endured until the pandemonium died. The seconds passed very slowly.

"Well," said Gore, wiping tears from the corners of his eyes, "let's get right down to business. What do each of you see as the central issue of this campaign? Let's start with you, Mrs. Cox."

The ensuing speech, bland and innocuous, was the highlight of the evening for Mimi Cox. After a few sentences about fiscal responsibility and the need for more social services, Dunwoody and Weinstein began ripping hunks of flesh from her exposed flanks.

"How insipidly naive," interrupted Weinstein when Cox made a point about the distribution of revenues among towns.

"What would you expect," chimed in Dunwoody, in rare agreement with Weinstein, "from someone who has never held elective office, who thinks that the state can be administrated like a Cub Scout den, and whose husband was recently seen emerging from the X-rated section of the Granville Video Gallery?"

It was a bloody spectacle, but one Darwin understood instantly. Cox never knew what hit her. As a Republican, she posed a clear alternative to Dunwoody, one who would get many votes out of sympathy and loyalty. The last opponent Weinstein wanted in the campaign was another woman to divide her own base of support. The two political pros wielded their knives as skillfully as fish mongers, and Cox was soon a stack of filets and a stripped carcass.

Darwin watched with morbid fascination, like he was watching the Vietnam War on the evening news. Gore seemed to be enjoying the action, but remembered occasionally that this was his show.

"And let's move along. Durwin, Durwin Huntman. You're the independent in this race. What do you see as the critical issue?"

Now it's my turn, thought Darwin. He smiled and braced himself for an attack like the one just witnessed. "Honesty," he said simply. "People need a leader who returns the trust of the voters."

"I could not agree more with my esteemed colleague," boomed Dunwoody, emphasizing his words with a fist pounded into an open palm. "Here's a guy who's up front about his lack of qualifications, who does not pretend that he knows what government is all about. He's not a refugee from the Junior League who thinks that the most pressing issue in the state is the preservation of Vermont's wild flowers."

Mimi Cox tried to defend herself by diverting attention

onto Darwin. "At least I am not a beer-swilling, dope-smoking sexual pervert whose own wife—"

"You're worse," snorted Weinstein, her thirst unsated. "You're a wimp. There's no other word for it. You represent the worst kind of oppressed woman, the one who is riding on the coattails of her husband's success."

During the commercial break Cox slumped to an amorphous mound of quivering flesh. No one noticed except Darwin. Gore was back at his medications, Weinstein at her note cards. The technicians scurried purposefully; Dunwoody massaged his temples. Darwin reached across Dunwoody to give Mimi's knee a reassuring squeeze, but she rebuked him with a non sequitur about the Symbionese Liberation Army.

The second half was calmer. Dunwoody and Weinstein mounted the soapbox for euphonius blusterings. Gore tried to provoke Darwin into recounting the seamiest low-lights of his Total Disclosure. Mimi Cox maintained a tight-lipped silence, making guttural noises from the back of her throat. She did not even acknowledge questions when directly addressed, resulting in awkward silences that Riley Gore filled with drivel about Sussex Junction. Eventually it wound to a close, Gore's smiling visage frozen on to a camera until someone called, "It's a wrap."

"That went well," said Dunwoody to Gore, who accepted the compliment by babbling to all around him:

"Good show. Very good show. I thought it went well. Super well. Good show. Heh-heh. Nailed it, didn't I? Terrific show. Way to go. Nice job, nice job."

Darwin helped Mimi Cox to her feet, but was elbowed out of the way by her husband, who spat out "Jackals!" as he led her away. Darwin removed his microphone clip and unthreaded it through his coat sleeve.

"Darwin, can you help me?" Natalie Weinstein had removed her microphone and was trying to work it down the beige, wool dress she was wearing. "I'm going to have to strip to get this thing out. And the idea of being exposed to the Riley Gores or Woody Dunwoody of the world makes me nauseous."

Darwin noted his own omission from the group of nauseating males and was vaguely pleased. "You seem pretty casual," he said, kneeling to tug at the cord exiting from her hemline, "for someone who has just participated in an execution."

"We're being kind to her. Woody and I talked about it earlier. We could either let her go through the extended agony and expense of a campaign, or we could be merciful and put her out of her misery now."

"So am I next?"

Weinstein laughed and gave her hips a shake so that the microphone droped into Darwin's hands. Her body was large-boned, but trim and angular. The sexist pig side of Darwin could not help but notice.

"No, Darwin. You're safe. You're harmless, a comic relief in the campaign. You'll draw a few votes from the lunatic fringe, but by and large you just give the incumbent and me more credibility. To most of the public you are a novelty. And they don't know if you are a John Bircher, a communist, or what. They just know you're a nut."

But Weinstein was wrong. If a vote was taken at that precise moment, with a public having seen Darwin talking casually to Dan Rather and then being the only nonparticipant in the savage attack on Mimi Cox, he would have been their choice. Only the supreme arrogance of Weinstein and Dunwoody kept them from even considering this possibility.

"Will you give me a ride home?" Weinstein's request struck Darwin as unusual. How many people came to a television taping with no provision for getting home? Darwin did not probe; Weinstein offered no explanation. He said sure.

They climbed into Darwin's Saab. A July day disappeared off to the west, over the Adirondacks. They had gone no farther than Manny and Marie's Quik-Stop when Natalie bade him stop. "Darwin, be a dear and buy me a beer." Never needing a second invation whenever beer was concerned, Darwin obeyed. Weinstein specified Labatt's Blue.

When Darwin was back in the car, she unscrewed a bottle for him, another for herself, and proposed a toast as they headed up the entrance ramp to Interstate 89.

"To the election. May the best man win."

"Power to the people," returned Darwin, and they clinked.

Darwin had now met Natalie Weinstein briefly on three or four occasions, but through her association with Sammi and her public presence, he felt as if he knew her quite well. Thirty-eight years old, a Brooklyn native, a graduate of City College of New York, she was swept northward by a romantic young husband who felt that the path to the future revolved around running a broken-down country inn in Bethel, Vermont. It was very romantic: nonstop repairs, wood hauling, sheet changing, and bill paying, interrupted periodically by the whimsical demands of tourists. On top of an overloaded schedule, Weinstein and her husband added the burden of child rearing (her daughter Caitlin was born in 1972) and self-sufficiency. There was always a garden producing green beans that needed canning (although they would never be eaten), and a Rototiller to be repaired.

Despite the fact that she was constantly anemic, chilly, and frazzled, Weinstein convinced herself that she was living the good life. Then, one October day during the height of leaf season, with an inn full of guests and a colicky baby, her husband announced that he was fed up. Moreover, he had fallen in love with a nineteen-year-old girl from the local tavern and they were heading south to Florida, where he had a job working construction.

Weinstein had not a clue to her husband's disaffection; she had been too busy. So she plodded on. Four years later Caitlin went off to school and Natalie sold the inn for a handsome profit. She used the proceeds to put herself through Vermont Law School. She worked in the district attorney's office for five years, then returned to the law school as a visiting professor.

Darwin got the whole life saga on the one-hour ride on Interstate 89, two and a half beers worth. This was hardly a side of Weinstein that he had expected, a sympathetic and vulnerable side. He felt his edgy stereotype fading faster than the twilight. He barely spoke on the ride, yet through his encouraging murmurs he knew that he had coaxed far more from Natalie Weinstein than either of them expected. He glanced over at her, seeing only the profile in the darkness. She had sunk back into the seat with her head against the rest, staring up at the sun visor as she talked.

She gave him directions to her home, a small contemporary perched on a hillside. "After the inn," she told him, "I never wanted to see an old house or eat anything homemade again. I've nearly succeeded."

The house was isolated up a long drive. A summer

house, really. Weinstein maintained an apartment in Montpelier for the school year. Caitlin was off at summer camp now. Darwin stopped, headlights shining on the front door.

"This has been better than therapy," she said, sitting upright. "C'mon in an have a glass of wine."

"I gotta go. I told Sunny I'd be back by nine-thirty."

"Dar-win." Weinstein's tone showed that she could see right through his feeble protest. "It's early, the kids are safe in bed, Sunny's planted in front of the television set, and I feel like I'm talking to a fellow adult for the first time in months. Indulge me, all right?"

The inside of Natalie Weinstein's was neat and fashionable, a mixture of antiques and wicker. It was the rarest of Vermont evenings, warm enough so that the screen doors to the deck were wide open. A June bug bashed comically against the screen.

"I'm getting out of this dress," said Natalie. "Pick out a bottle of wine from the rack in the kitchen and put on some music."

Darwin flipped through her compact disks. "Yuppie music," he sneered. "I only do rock and roll, and now's not the time. Let's listen to the night." And the crickets played magnificently.

He picked out a Cabernet Sauvignon that he mentally priced at twelve dollars a bottle, uncorked it, found the appropriate glasses, and settled onto the wicker sofa. He tasted the wine, rich and complex, and his discomfort grew. It skyrocketed when Weinstein entered the room wearing a sheer, flowing negligee that looked entirely appropriate to the mood and setting. She joined him on the sofa. He was now immobile.

She looked into his face as she sipped the wine: "I took a big chance dressing like this."

Darwin smiled and nodded. "I know. I've got to go."

"I've scared you away by being too aggressive, haven't I?"

"No, your aggression is fine. In fact, it's perfect." Darwin gave himself the luxury of a long, uninhibited look at the length of her body, a look she accepted without flinching. "It's the situation."

"You mean Sammi? Darwin, I don't think she's coming back to you. There's too much bitterness there."

Darwin hated the cool confidence with which she spoke. "I don't accept that. But besides Sammi, it's also this campaign and my entire life. I'm the wonderful guy who brought you Total Disclosure, remember?"

Weinstein laughed, not a snort of derision, but lightly therapeutic. "I've thought a lot about you and Total Disclosure. For the longest time I could not tell if you were sincere or just innovatively manipulative."

"What did you decide?"

"Sincere."

"What decided it for you?"

"You remember that part of your speech where you told about the time you were twelve years old and you went out hunting with your bow and arrow? You killed your neighbor's cat, then never told anyone?"

"Right."

"Well, I checked out the story."

"And?"

"You did have a neighbor who did have a cat that inexplicably disappeared twenty-eight years ago. I'd say the story is true."

"I can show you where the body is buried. I carried that burden around too long."

"We can all benefit from unburdening. You just have a creative way of accomplishing it. I'm more traditional."

She hitched herself closer, her face inches from his, so that he could feel her breath. Her hand rested lightly on his abdomen, and his body began to betray him. "Oh Darwin, Mr. Total Disclosure. Dis-clothes me!"

Her aura drew him down and around, but Darwin steadied himself, placing a hand on the back of the sofa and lifting himself to his feet. Standing directly in front of her, his words were vintage Hunter:

"It is a far, far better thing that I do, than I have ever done—"

"No, dummy, if it's a far better rest you are looking for, then get back down on this couch. This is no time to get noble."

Weinstein took his hand and pulled gently. She spoke deliberately, one word at a time so that there could be no mistaking the meaning: "Let me try a slightly different tack. What does a healthy, mature woman need to do to get laid on a night like this?" All of Darwin's willpower was devoted to his resistance. There was no energy left for speaking. She leaned forward and brushed a light kiss onto his crotch.

"In high school we called it 'pitching a tent,' or sometimes 'pulling a Pinocchio.' "

"See, you cannot tell a lie. You want me, you can have me, so take me."

"No, I'm taking what little resolve I have left and leaving while there is still time."

"What's 'resolve' anyway?"

" 'Resolve' is a fluid substance that normally resides in the brain, but during moments of passion descends to engorge the penis."

Weinstein took a sip of her wine. "You're not really going to leave me with this beautiful night and a bottle of wine?"

Darwin nodded weakly.

"Why don't you make mad, passionate love to me first, then tell the world tomorrow?"

"You know I wouldn't."

"Men," said Weinstein sadly. "Who needs them?" She sighed, and released him. Darwin turned to go. At the doorway he turned back.

"I don't give rain checks," she preempted him.

Darwin sagged. "Are we that predictable?"

She nodded, and shooed him away with a flip of her hand.

10

(Yet Another) Rural Roar

Slinging Stevie Mugford came to town on the last day of July and was recognized instantly by nine-year-old Duke Hunter. Darwin came home from work to find his son and Sunny Moss shooting hoops with a Boston Celtic.

Seeing a real basketball player on a Vermont-style court was humorous, if not pathetic. The hoop was nine inches short of regulation, tilted at forty-five degrees, with only a few tatters to remind of where the net had been. The ball was true enough, but dribbling on a court with random tufts of grass added a new variable to the game.

"Don't worry," answered Mugford to Sunny's apology for dribbling conditions that caused the ball to occasionally bounce at right angles, "even the parquet in the Garden has a few soft spots. We call it 'home-court advantage.' "

At thirty-five, Mugford was the elder statesman of the Celtics. Darwin expected a feeble old horse, but instead found a six-foot-five stallion, five years younger than himself. Practically a kid. Mugford was in Vermont to appear at the Red Auerbach basketball summer camp at Montpelier Community College. While in the area, he reasoned, he should meet the lady whose goat-milk yogurt had been instrumental in the Celtic's march to the championship. He came to Upper Granville unannounced, and finding no one home at the Clarke residence, decided to pass some time with Duke and Sunny.

Darwin offered him a beer, which he accepted. Then they sat at the picnic table in the backyard, awaiting the return of Sue Clarke.

Since his playoff heroics, Mugford had basked in so much adulation that his needs for reality had been completely neglected. Vermont, and especially Upper Granville, were so soothing, so genuine, so . . . he searched for the word, settled for *real*.

"It's unbelievable," he said, feeling relaxed amid the vernal hillsides, "but after a while you can't remember who you really are. You're not sure if you're who *you* think you are, or who *everyone else* thinks you are, or who the last reporter thinks you are. You don't know if people like you for yourself or because they've seen you on TV. People buy you drinks, girls want to fuck you, everyone wants a little piece of you."

"Remind me," answered Darwin, "never to sink eleven in a row during the playoffs."

Emil Dummerston Weed arrived in his pickup. Bad news, he said. Weinstein and Dunwoody had escaped from their pens and were plundering Martha Gunion's flower garden. "We need to catch them."

"Who are Weinstein and Dunwoody?" asked Mugford.

"Our pigs," explained Darwin. "They're adolescents, meaning they're fast, strong, and crazy, kind of like Charles Barkley."

He got up to go. Mugford offered his assistance, which was immediately accepted, and the three men climbed into Emil's truck.

Emil was captain of this maneuver. The pigs were grazing peacefully in the Gunion's vegetable garden when they arrived. Martha Gunion was lying in a swoon on the porch, being fanned by Walt. "Do something," he pleaded. "They've already eaten the nasturtiums and phlox. I don't know what we'll do if they get the hydrangea."

Emil got down on one knee and mapped out with a stick in the dirt a flanking movement whereby Darwin and Slingin' Stevie would cut off escape routes while he would herd the swine onto a jutting peninsula by the pond. Then they would close ranks and go for the capture. After hearing the plan, Mugford said, "Aren't we making this too complicated? Can't we just go down there and grab'em?"

Emil affixed a five-second stare onto him. The look said: "I won't tell you how to defense Dominique Wilkins if you don't tell me how to catch a pig."

Mugford quickly understood and threw up his hands in conciliation. "I withdraw the question!" he said with a laugh.

The plan worked like a charm, and soon the three men had the two pigs trapped with no route of escape. "Okay," said Emil. "Now be smart. These suckers'll amaze you with how fast they are."

The pigs were either oblivious to the approach of the men or completely unconcerned. They waited until their captors were three feet away, then in one squealingly orgasmic second, one dove into the water while the other made like Bo Jackson and burst through Mugford and Darwin, leaving the two men unsure whether to laugh or cry.

"Good job, men," said Emil sarcastically.

"What do we do now, coach?" asked a sheepish Mugford.

"First we'll get the one in the pond." The pig had gone to the center and was swimming in circles. "We need a volunteer to go in there and herd him out to us on the edge." There was silence, finally broken by Emil: "I'd do it, but someone has to grab the piggy when he comes out, and you two turkeys have already shown you can't cut it."

"I'll do it," said Mugford.

"Thank God," said a relieved Darwin, "I couldn't think of an excuse."

Mugford stripped naked, causing a second swoon from Martha Gunion, and waded into the pond. Go right for him, said Emil. Yeah, chipped in Darwin, show him who's boss. Mugford took a few tentative strokes through the algae-laden water, attracting the pig's attention with his splashing. The pig saw Mugford and did the logical thing—he charged. Mugford, all six-foot-five of him, thrashed wildly out of the pond, squealing louder than the pig.

When the laughter died down, they opted for the Hunter Plan. Open the door to the pen, fill the trough with fresh grain and tasty morsels of garbage, then drink Walt's beer on the porch, hoping the pigs decided to return. Worked like a charm.

Sue Clarke's Plymouth Voyager with its painted IN YO' FACE YOGURT logo was in the driveway upon their return. Darwin walked Slinging Stevie over and introduced them. Sue was suitably unimpressed, and subjected both men to an extended treatise on what a mental case her husband Townshend had become. Darwin excused himself, saying:

"Sue, I'm leaving. I've heard it all before."

Mugford found her ire refreshing, and within a week they were lovers. Every night, after the campers had been fed suppers and run lay-up drills, Slinging Stevie came to town. Townshend, when he was in town, was rushing about in such a continual haze of self-importance that he never noticed. There was always a planning board to be courted, an agency to meet with, an architect, a consultant.

The campaign was now in the trenches. Darwin walked carefully planned routes from prefab to doublewide, shaking hands and passing time with the residents of the Fifth District. His message was simple. Vote, and vote for whom you trust. A vote for Darwin is a vote against hypocrisy.

Darwin tried, above all else, to be personable in his visits. Many times his reputation preceded him and he had to correct notions that he was either a left-wing fiend or Riley Gore's best friend. He campaigned for an hour each morning and two at night. On weekends he packed a picnic lunch and took the kids on cross-country hand-pumping outings, stopping in gores and hollows that had never seen a real-live politician.

All in all, he thought, the campaign was progressing well. He was working hard and efficiently. People responded. Even so, he suspected he was losing ground. There were no pollsters to consult, only the hunches that one developed talking to people outside the grocery store or at the sanitary landfill. Dunwoody could pick and choose appearances to achieve maximum visibility. Weinstein had perfected the art of networking, with a spider-work of whale lovers and peace mongers at her beck and call. Darwin's "machine" was no more than the fervor of

Teresa Blanchard, the ingenuity of Captain Goo-Roo, and his own willingness to pound the turf.

Mimi Cox had resurfaced, not as a candidate, but as the founder and chairperson for the League of American Decency (LOAD), a coalition of whites, Anglo-Saxons, and Protestants, from all walks of upper-middle-class life, whose goal was to return the nation to the values of its founders.

After her humiliation on *Straddlin' the Fence*, Cox had gone into two weeks of seclusion (actually she went to a very expensive drug-and-alcohol rehabilitation center in Southern California). She emerged with the fire of the reborn. Her passion was directed not at returning to the political fray, nor was it directed at those who had brought her down. Surprisingly, her bile was focused on Darwin Hunter. If there was a purpose to the LOAD other than to ensure the nonelection of Darwin, no one could see it.

"Why," Darwin asked General Beauregard while both sat contemplatively in his study one night, "are all the women in my life berserk?"

Darwin was as puzzled by the opposition of Mimi Cox as he was by the support of Teresa Blanchard. Teresa continued her rabid support of the Hunter candidacy, mobilizing bedrock native energy. "That's what is so great about Darwin," she told a gathering of work-at-home knitters. "He doesn't believe in much of anything, except honesty. He does not have a platform or ties to special interest groups. He just does whatever is right. He's the politician for people who hate politicians!"

The logic appealed to a surprising number of people. Darwin himself did not understand Teresa or what motivated her. He never asked for her assistance, nor had he nurtured it in any way. He felt awkward that, in a campaign based on honesty, she was the one person who knew of the most significant omission in his Total Disclosure, his one night liaison with her at the Tunbridge Fair three years earlier. Was her allegiance gratitude for his discretion? Or was it rooted in fear, the fruit of reverse blackmail? She provided no clues. The only meaningful dialogue that passed between them was at a 4-H convention where Teresa had wrangled a keynote speaker's role for Darwin. He did his generic speech, an update of the Total Disclosure theme. Afterward she caught his eye, smiled, winked, and said:

"You may be honest, but you're not dumb."

As much as he tried, Darwin could not understand her meaning. When he guessed, he did not like the answer. His unease grew, even as Teresa campaigned on, infused with the spirit of a true believer. She balanced duties as a mother, wife, and cosmetologist, discovering within herself new wells of resource. She neglected nothing, not her chores, not her children, not her husband, and yet nothing so threatened her relationship with Bennett as this newfound competence.

Bennett Blanchard was even more uneasy than Darwin. In recent years Bennett had watched Teresa become an authorized agent for Tupperware, Amway products, and Mary Kay Cosmetics. Although he found these pursuits trivial, as he did all pursuits that did not revolve specifically around the operation of the Blanchard Farm, they had the redeeming quality of providing welcome cash. But for his wife to devote so much time and energy to promote the political career of a transient Flatlander—it did not make sense. Bennett spent uncounted hours brooding over the situation as he delivered endless loads of manure, as he mowed and baled hay, as he listened to the milking machines at night in the barn. It just didn't make sense.

Bennett considered talking to Emil about the situation, but Emil would turn the situation into a barnyard razz. Bennett once commented that he considered Farrah Fawcett-Majors a "real piece of gear," and for two years endured insinuations that he was about to leave the farm in search of the golden-haired goddess. He might have tried his father, but his dad had slowed down this last year, and Bennett did not want to concern him about anything outside the farm. With continued low milk prices and those fools Townshend and Walt trying to run them off their own land, Bennett did not want to further burden his father with domestic disharmony. So he brooded on, wondering why and how his simple life had become so complicated.

Trust U.S. fell on difficult times once the blush of the initial publicity faded. The great idea to salvage history from the tinsel-strewn sidewalks of twentieth-century America ran afoul of planning boards, bureaucrats, Act 250, displaced farmers, and rabid environmentalists. Townshend and Walt were disheartened to see themselves portrayed as ham-fisted plunderers of the North. At a town meeting a woman compared them to the slaughterers of the baby harp seals. "But we are the *good* guys!" insisted Townshend. As time went by, however, fewer people were inclined to believe them.

Nor had the town residents proved as susceptible to the allure of big bucks as the entrepreneurs anticipated. Darwin had not agreed to sell, and the Blanchards showed no crack in their united veneer. Townshend maintained an upbeat appearance, but Walt was clearly losing interest.

Hell's bells, it was his wife's family money anyway, and a million or so lost would hardly be noticed. Most of all, Walt needed topics of conversation for the after-dinner portion of ARFO meetings, and this one was wearing thin.

The lack of progress was of more significance to Townshend. He was not concerned financially, but from an identity standpoint, this was his big move in life. This was what coming to Vermont, the years of scraping by as a carpenter's helper and roof shoveler, had prepared him for. This was Fate, and Townshend was not about to abandon a dream.

His ability to maintain buoyancy, however, was negatively impacted by the gradual realization that a six-foot-five-inch Boston Celtic was stealing his wife. Townshend and Sue, as a couple, had been comatose for some time. Confronting even the obvious was now difficult. He had burned bridges with most of his friends. Even Darwin was too busy coping with his own marital problems to be of help. But as much as he tried to ignore the situation, it refused to go away.

Darwin drove out of Upper Granville on a soft August morning. There were two dairy farms on the north side of Center Granville that he wanted to hit on his way to work. He was in a good mood. It was a nice day. In his stomach burbled the composite of his favorite summer breakfast—cantaloupe, whole wheat toast, and coffee. His gut was relieved of accumulated waste.

He waved to Hoyt Blanchard, seated on a stump just outside the family dairy farm. Darwin ruminated on waves. A wave in the Northland was as distinctive as a face. Tina Pisano waved as if she was saying bon voyage from the fantail of the cruise ship. Joe, on the other hand, had a practiced, single finger off the top of his steering wheel. Bennett waved with his head, an unsmiling toss backward, while Emil waved by making an exaggerated expression of surprise on his face. It was the same expression that some of the stars on *Hollywood Squares* used when their names were announced.

Darwin stopped midway down the hill and did a U-turn. His reverie had been interrupted by the belated recognition of something unusual. He frequently passed Hoyt Blanchard on his way out of town, but he had never, ever seen Hoyt in any posture but bustling in a grizzled farmer way to the next chore. Something was wrong.

Hoyt was still seated on the stump. Darwin got out and saw that Hoyt was paler than skim milk. His hat was lying next to him, and a fine bead of sweat coated his forehead. His right hand was flat against his chest. Instantly Darwin knew that Hoyt was experiencing a heart attack.

"Hello, Hoyt," Darwin said, trying not to sound alarmed. "Having trouble breathing?" Hoyt tried to answer but settled for a nod. "Bennett in the barn?" Another nod. Darwin streaked into the barn. Bennett was at the far end, trying to maneuver a cow to its stanchion.

"Bennett, your dad's having a heart attack. C'mon!" Darwin turned to return to the older man.

Bennett did not even look up from his chore. "It's just a spell. He'll be fine in a minute."

"I tell you it's a heart attack and he needs to get to a hospital, now."

Darwin ran back to Hoyt, who had not budged.

"My arm is numb," gasped Hoyt.

"Let's go, big guy," Darwin said reassuringly, dipping down and putting Hoyt's arm around his shoulder. "We're going to get this checked out at the hospital." He was almost to the front seat of the car when Bennett showed up at the barn door.

"I'm not letting you take my father to the hospital. If he needs to go, his family can take him."

"Bennett, it doesn't matter who takes him, so long as he gets there, and soon."

"Well, I'm taking him! Soon's I finish milking."

Darwin was as urgent as Bennett was stubborn. "We don't have time to argue. It makes sense for me to take him. I'm a doctor and I know everyone at the hospital. You gather up the family and meet us there."

"Maybe you didn't hear me—" began Bennett. He was stopped short by a wave from his father. The two of them had to strain to hear Hoyt's words:

"Let him take me."

Darwin plodded by rote through the morning, and when his eleven o'clock patient was late, called the hospital. Hoyt was in intensive care, his condition listed as stable. He could not accept phone calls but would be able to see visitors later in the day.

After his last appointment Darwin called Sunny to say that he would be late and to go ahead and feed the kids. He thought to bring something to Hoyt but couldn't decide what was appropriate for a laid-up dairy farmer. Chocolates? Flowers? Girlie magazines? Finally he decided on a small tin of bag balm, the universal panacea for everything from chafed udders to infections. Little bag balm on the old chest. Fix you right up, Darwin thought.

He checked in at the nurse's station, learning that his diagnosis of a heart attack was correct, but that the prognosis for recovery was good. Hoyt's appearance was not as good as the prognosis, however. His skin had the distant grayness of November skies. He was alert, however, and his eyes met Darwin's quickly.

"Hello, Darwin." His voice was placid, possibly even content.

"Looks like you're going to live to milk another day. How are you feeling?"

"Compared to what?"

"Don't pull that corny old Vermonter stuff on me. Really, how do you feel?"

"Like an old man."

"Here's some miracle cure." Darwin handed him the green tin of bag balm. "It'll cure what ails ya. Stella been here?"

"You just missed her. She went back to fix supper for the boys."

"Bennett?"

"Not yet. He'll be in by and by."

"Anything I can do for you?"

"Open the window."

Hoyt's gaze was focused vaguely beyond the pane. Darwin opened the large frame and let in the sounds and smells of summer. The same soft breeze of the morning washed over them, bringing with it the smell of grass and the sounds of birds singing out their territories. Darwin noticed that Hoyt had closed his eyes. He prepared to make a silent exit, but before he could rise, Hoyt spoke:

"I want to talk, Darwin. And I don't need anyone to say nuthin', but just listen.

"I was born in the same house where I now live in 1909, the year they stopped making Indian-head pennies. There was seven of us—Mama, Father, my older brother Alton, and my three sisters, Enis, Edna, and Myrtie. Everyone's dead now 'cept me, an' I'm almost, and Enis, who lives in Albany, New York.

"The community was different. Everyone was a farmer. Even the preacher and the sawyer who ran the mill by Tomar Brook farmed on the side. The farms were smaller, and all the land was clear. You could stand by the schoolhouse where that old lady jogger lives and not see a tree, 'cept for the stands of sugar maples. We raised more crops then. Had to, 'cuz if you couldn't grow it, catch it, make it, or kill it, you jus' did without.

"The only cash crop we had was charcoal. We'd stack the logs in a pyramid and let'em smolder till they were black and dry. We sold the charcoal to a man from Hartford who bought it to fire the furnaces in a foundry for making cast-iron radiators. I remember my childhood as being near perfect, fluffy snowstorms, and fresh-baked rolls, and sugar on snow.

"The Depression came, but it didn't mean much to us, because we'd always been in a depression. There was no money in the valley. You wanted something, you traded something. You could trade deer hides for boots and gloves. Potatoes could get you anything from sugar to whiskey. We didn't miss money at all, least not growing up. The girls' dresses may have been made from grain sacks, but it didn't matter none, because so's were everybody's.

"Stella came to be the schoolmarm in 1930. She lived one month with one family, then moved on to the next. We didn't get exposed to lots of ladyfolk, but it always seemed that things fell into place. Stella and I both knew right away that we was meant to be.

"I said earlier that there weren't no money in town.

There weren't no money in Vermont. It weren't uncommon in those days for one or more of a family's young men to go off and earn money to send home. This made particular sense for me, seeing as where I was thinking of taking Stella and starting a place of my own. 'Course, Alton was good for nilly nuthin', but he was oldest, so it was decided that I would go. Jobs were scarce as hen's teeth, but Oakley McBean's father had a brother who ran a textile plant in New Bedford, and he got me a position there."

Hoyt stopped, letting the sounds of summer wash over them both. The sounds got louder, Darwin noticed, as the light grew dimmer. Why had it taken him forty years to notice that? The story must be over, he thought. His past relationship with Hoyt, while pleasant, had usually been limited to a few sentences, usually about the weather. He felt privileged to be sharing so much of the man's life. To Darwin's pleasure and surprise, the story continued:

"I only been out of Vermont once."

"In 1919. A trip to Fenway Park, where you saw Babe Ruth play," interjected Darwin.

Hoyt beamed. "That's right. Naturally, I was a little scared to be in a big city like New Bedford, surrounded by strangers, who didn't even speak English. The work didn't bother me none. They had me fixing machines, which comes natural to me anyway. And the work weren't hard. Lord, after you've worked a farm, no work seems hard.

"Things went on fine, 'cept I was the loneliest boy in New England. I didn't like that city. Didn't like the weather, much colder'n Vermont. No snow. Didn't like the people either. For a young farm boy like me, New Bedford was the end of the world. 'Course I wrote home every week, and sent my money, but I was just counting the weeks till I could go home."

Up to this point in the story Hoyt had spoken as if in a reverie, his eyes closed or gazing on the white ceiling. Now he turned to Darwin and held out a grizzled hand to touch Darwin's knee.

"But the truth is, Darwin, I took up with a woman, a Portagee woman from the Cape Verde Islands. Her name was Rosa Marquita Gomes. Ro-sa Mar-qui-ta Gom-es. She was older'n me by four or five years. She worked in the factory where I fixed machines. Her husband was killed a year earlier when the fishing boat he worked on went down in a storm. I suppose she was just as lonely as me.

"She didn't speak the best English, but I didn't have any trouble understanding her. She asked me up to her house on Periwinkle Way for tea. She kept that place as neat as a pin. I can see it now—sunlight shining through the windows onto a china tea set she got for her wedding. Hot teas, with lemon and sugar cookies.

"I didn't see it the same as courtin'. I was already betrothed to Stella. Still, I started having tea more'n more with my 'Quita, and pretty soon we were living as husband and wife. I won't say that those were the best two years of my life, but I will say that no human being has ever gived another the warmth and comfort that she gave me.

"I'd always said that when my time was done, I'd be going back to Vermont. But then the time came, and I started wondering. I thought about it every which way. I couldn't see myself fixin' machines in a New Bedford factory for the rest of my life, but I couldn't see her on the farm in Upper Granville neither.

"Finally, just before I was about to go home, I made up my mind and I asked to take her hand. But you know what? She wouldn't have me! She said she had to live by the sea, but that she knew farming was in my blood. We were just not intended, she said.

"I asked her every way I knew how, but she just kept saying no. So I come back, married Stella, and took over the farm when it proved Alton was more interested in writin' books than milkin' cows. And I've never told no one this story, Darwin, and there's one more thing to tell, 'cuz when I left my 'Quita I was sure she was with child. She never told me, so I never knew fer sure. But she was. I knew it, but I never even wrote. Wouldn'ta done no good. I jus' left it all behind me."

Darwin fidgeted. "And so, now, do you want to know?"

Hoyt closed his eyes. "I don't know if I want to know. I just wanted to tell someone." And he was asleep.

The attack was minor. After three days in the hospital Hoyt came home. He was thin and drawn and looked strange in his coveralls. The farm was now Bennett's. Without ceremony, without proclamation, without a word, the mantle was passed from one generation to the next.

Two weeks later, on a Sunday twilight, Darwin was rewarding himself for another hard day of flesh pressing by wallowing in the Sunday papers. He certainly had become sedate in his dotage. Was it the absence of Sammi, the increased parental responsibilities, middle age, or the time of man? He could not remember the last time he caroused. Even his encounters with Captain Goo-Roo were businesslike.

The charcoal was lit. The beer was perfect. The kids were watching the *Disney Sunday Movie*. Darwin reviewed a few days of neglected mail. Suddenly there was the familiar metallic dink-dink-dink that he had heard on a cold fall day months before. He looked up to see Townshend Clarke, accompanied by both his children, pounding a property marker into the same spot. Seconds later he heard the sound of Bennett Blanchard's tractor coughing to life.

"Here we go," said Darwin, toasting the valley with his beer. "Yet another rural roar."

Townshend had descended to the roadside by the time Bennett arrived. They did not speak. Bennett charged by him, toward the stake. Townshend grabbed something from his car, then charged after. Darwin was horrorstruck. He had a pistol.

The tableau unfolded in miniature, silent toys on a lush, green hillside in full bloom of summer glory. Bennett pulled out the stake and, as he had done before, threw it into the woods. Descending the hill, he encountered Townshend. There was shouting. Darwin could hear the words, but the tone was enough to recognize the universal threatening babble of men on the verge of confrontation. Townshend pointed the gun. Darwin was motionless, paralyzed, stupefied. There was a frozen instant, a tableau of disbelief, then Bennett slapped the gun out of Townshend's hands. There was a flash as the gun hit the ground. A second later the report rang through the valley. The echo was followed by the sound of a child crying. Heather Clarke, six years old, had been hit.

The men were shaken from their tussle. The girl was standing, clutching herself just below the nape of her neck. Townshend was moving aimlessly, Bennett moving toward the girl. Darwin ran. The wineglass serenity of the valley lay in glistening shards.

After performing enough first aid to know that the wound was not life threatening, Darwin drove Townshend and Heather to the hospital, then stayed through the treatment and the ensuing police reports. The police bandied about charges of "assault with a deadly weapon," and "aggravated assault with intent to kill," but in the end there were no charges, due to Bennett Blanchard's refusal to file a complaint.

Heather was checked into the hospital for the night, her mother by her side. Sue refused even to acknowledge her husband. Darwin drove Townshend home. They were silent. As they entered the dirt road leading to Upper Granville, the forest enveloped them, its shimmering canopy hiding the moonlit summer sky.

"You're very lucky," said Darwin, "that there were no charges."

"No charges," mumbled Townshend. "Only a child who's scarred for life."

Darwin looked at his friend in the darkness and tried to remember what he looked like with his ponytail. Had it really been so long ago? Had it really been so long ago that the world was intact?

"I'll stay with you tonight," Darwin said.

11

The Captain at the Wheel

Amid the furor, the march of the seasons carried on. The maples in front of the Clarkes' showed the first slash of color. The end of summer was upon the valley.

Almost a decade before (God, had it been that long?) the first annual Running of the Valley was held to determine who—Darwin Hunter or Bruce Liebermann, the Stowe Stallion—was the swifter, more obstinate, pigheaded, and egotistical. The challenge was issued on New Year's Eve and settled on Labor Day. No one remembered who won. More important than the winner was the establishment of a tradition. After the success of the first event, the community put aside hostilities and mundane considerations for one day, Labor Day, in recognition of the passage of the friendliest season. A cathartic Running of the Valley punctuated the summer, enabling children to return to school and the adults to face winter without a sense of loss.

The Stowe Stallion was now gone. The Running of the Valley had experienced highs and lows in terms of community participation, but in spite of the strange paths that individual lives had taken, no one for a second considered ignoring the event. Hannah Duncan and Tina Pisano had ambitious ideas. Coincidentally, they were the only two serious runners left, the jogging craze having passed the way of Euell Gibbons and the Strawberry Alarm Clock. Darwin was in no shape to challenge for the throne he once held, but vowed to be there with Adidases on when the starting gun sounded. When Hannah called to say that she was mobilizing the community, Darwin was skeptical.

"There's a little too much bad blood in this community, especially after the Bennett-Townshend affair. This might be like putting red-throated male sticklebacks in the same goldfish bowl," he warned.

"I don't think so," said Hannah. "I've talked to a few people, and they're up for it. I even talked to Sammi, and she's coming down."

"Great," said Darwin, trying to sound casual. "I wonder if she'll bring Georgio?" Hannah did not correct him.

Darwin had been too busy running a different kind of race to worry about conditioning. He thought nostalgically about days when he could devote himself to staving off middle age. Now the war was lost, and he could content himself instead with being the busiest and most important man in the world, a title he shared with Bennett Blanchard, Townshend Clarke, Walt Gunion, Howard "Warren" Pease, Joe Pisano, and Gimp Fenvessey. He tried to achieve the best of both worlds by trying a few campaign routes on foot, but it was difficult to achieve credibility dressed in short pants and running shoes.

Fortune smiled on Darwin once again. The last week of August was cold and raw, even by Vermont standards.

Darwin was tramping house to house, continuing the odyssey designed to bring him to Montpelier and inner peace. He approached a rambling frame farmhouse. A wisp of smoke from the chimney bespoke life inside, and yet no one answered Darwin's knock. He was about to leave a campaign flyer and continue on his rounds when he noticed smoke inside the house. He tried the door latch. Not locked. He entered.

The reek of smoke was noxious, and its origin obvious. Visibility was limited, but Darwin discovered the source of the fire when he came close to falling through the smoldering floor just in front of the stove. Embers had escaped and ignited the floor.

He ran to the kitchen, drew a pot of water, ran back, threw it on the fire, and immediately realized that the rate at which the fire was spreading was much faster than his ability to fetch water. Darwin found a phone and called the fire department, gave them directions, and asked helplessly, "What do I do?"

"Get out!" came the reply.

Darwin did not heed the advice, but instead ran about in a frenzy, looking for a fire extinguisher, or a hose, or something. In the mud room he found the something, a chain saw. His mind was as clear as the air in the house. Thinking back, he realized what an imprudent decision he made, but to his credit, he made it quickly.

The chain saw not only had gas, an improbability in itself, but it started on the first pull—the first time in recorded history that this had ever happened in Vermont. Without hesitation Darwin began cutting the floor around the smoldering hole.

Now, flying wood chips and mechanical din were added to the fray. This is really intelligent, thought Darwin, having signed on for the duration. The floor is ready to burst into flames, and I'm standing here holding a container of gasoline. But he kept wailing away, adrenaline coursing through his veins as fast as the chain around the blade.

The smoldering hole fell onto the dirt floor of the cellar with a reassuring whumpf. The monster that, moments before, threatened to burst into a conflagration, now lay harmlessly one floor below. Darwin turned off the chain saw and listened to the blood pound in his head as he gaped at the hole. From upstairs he heard footsteps, and turned toward the stairwell in time to see a bent woman in her eighties, standing in terror. "What's that?" she said, seeing the hole in her floor. "What's that?"

The next few minutes were as confusing as the previous few, Darwin trying to introduce himself to the woman and to explain the hole in the living room floor while fire engines burst into the driveway, sirens ablare. The firemen ushered Darwin and the lady outside. A man came running out of the woods, his look of panic identifying him immediately as the homeowner.

"Mother!" he cried, rushing to the old lady.

"This man cut a big hole in our floor!" she exclaimed.

Holy shit, thought Darwin. This guy would get on his case for cutting a hole in his floor. The fire chief, who stood with them, admiring the efficient work of his charges, came to Darwin's rescue.

"This man," he said to the newcomer, "saved your house, and your mother."

The newspapers made a hero of Darwin. CANDIDATE SAVES HOUSE, MOM, said the *Burlington Free Press*. TOTAL DISCLOSURE ADVOCATE THWARTS FIRE, headlined the Granville *Clarion*. The next day, however, Darwin plunged back into the rigors of the campaign fray. Heroism was quickly forgotten when two of the women in the campaign came into conflict.

Teresa Blanchard versus Mimi Cox was the classic match up, the brawler and the stylist, two invincible ladies charging head-on.

The occasion was the Central Vermont Teachers Convocation. Every year, just prior to the beginning of school, area teachers gathered to plan curricula, discuss mutual problems, and listen to speakers of interest. Darwin was invited.

He arrived and immediately saw the potential for trouble. Teresa and Mimi were jawboning at the entrance to the Granville Elementary School. Cox was carrying a placard that read, DARWIN DOES THE DEVILS WORK. Several other League of American Decency volunteers were with her, brandishing signs reading A.B.D.! (ANYBODY BUT DARWIN) and TOTAL DISCLOSURE IS TOTAL EXPOSURE.

Teresa had her own band of loyalists, with their signs reading DAIRYMEN FOR DARWIN, DARWIN HUNTER FIRST OF A NEW BREED, and (Darwin winced) VOTE YOUR HEART, VOTE DARWIN!

The decibel level was high, the tone shrill, and Darwin considered it even more foolhardy than chain sawing through a burning floor when he stepped in between the shouting ladies. Mimi suggested to Teresa that she was under some Satanic spell. Teresa made a lunge for Cox, but Darwin intercepted her. He held her firmly by the shoulders, as he would a small child, making sure eye contact was achieved before he said:

"Teresa, we don't want trouble. Don't you see that nothing would serve their cause as much as provoking an incident from us?"

Teresa's look softened and she said, "You are *so* wise."

Darwin suppressed momentary nausea as she turned quietly and led her followers away. He turned to Cox, who stared at him, wild-eyed. "Howyadoin', Mimi? Shouldn't you be holding out a wooden cross." No response. He continued: "Hey, there is one question I've got to ask you. On that TV show, Gore, Weinstein, and Dunwoody made fun of you. They tossed you back and forth, beat you to a bloody pulp and then left you to die. So why me? Why am I the one you direct your anger at?"

Cox's expression tightened, as if someone had grabbed a fistful of skin from in back of her head and pulled her face tight against her skull. Her voice, when it finally came, was a guttural growl:

"Because . . . you . . . touched . . . me!"

"Oh," said Darwin in his dinkiest tone. He gave a little nod and left, remembering the light touch on his opponent's knee, intended to communicate sympathy and support. This woman, he thought, is beyond therapy.

Darwin made a brief speech to the teachers, after which the floor was opened to questions. The Cox and Blanchard factions were separated widely enough in the audience that Darwin felt the chances of confrontation were minimal. He took some innocuous questions from the floor, like where did he stand on pay increases for teachers and what color were Dan Rather's eyes, when the first blood-roiling issue surfaced:

"What is your position on mandatory seat-belt usage?" Vermonters loved to dwell on this issue, most of them feeling that personal liberties inside the auto were more sacred than within the bedroom. Darwin knew that this heavily liberal audience would support such regulation, but saw no point to mince words:

"I think it's bullshit."

"How about gun control?"

"Bullshit."

The boos were now audible, although countered effectively by a smattering of applause.

"How about the bottle deposit law?"

"Bullshit."

"The Equal Rights Amendment?"

"Moose crap."

Darwin had accomplished what he did best, to stir the emotions of his constituency. There were mini-debates going on throughout the hall. "Mob rule," chuckled Darwin. He let it continue for a moment, then called for, and was able to restore, order.

"Don't you see?" he began. "This is democracy in action. You're getting to speak your pieces rather than listening to me drone on. When it comes time to vote, your basic decision comes down to what you want: Someone to represent you, or someone to lead? For me the question is: Do I do what you tell me to do, or do what I think is right? I want it clear where I stand. I will listen, but when the roll call comes, I will follow my conscience, no matter who hoots and hollers."

Mimi Cox stood to be recognized. Darwin nodded to her, and after identifying herself, she launched into an extended explanation of the League of American Decency and how it stood for the restoration of traditional values. Did Darwin Hunter, she asked, support traditional values?

"Am I for traditional values? You mean like in 1776 when the vote of a black man counted for three fifths of the vote of a white man, and women could not vote at all? No, I'm not for that."

His avoidance of an obvious trap drew applause from the audience, but failed to derail the Cox express.

"Let's forget the clever rhetoric, Mr. Hunter, you've openly disclosed your many sins under the guise of truthfulness, so tell us the truth now. Why do you do the Devil's work?"

Darwin, normally quick with a retort, did not have a chance to open his mouth before Teresa Blanchard was on her feet:

"I'll answer that. The man does not portray himself as God, as do most politicians. He's human, and he's done things that are human, and he's man enough to admit it."

"And who's this?" Cox had tossed the bait cleverly and was now about to set the hook. "A woman devoted to a man who is not her husband?"

"Are you suggesting—" shrieked Teresa.

"Yes, I am suggesting."

Women have well-honed killer instincts, thought Darwin. Whoever invented the phrase about being caught between a rock and a hard place had never been caught between two self-righteous women.

"You're saying we're having an affair?" Teresa's voice was subdued but projected well enough that everyone in the audience of two hundred could hear each syllable.

"Yes, I am."

"All right, let's put it to the test." Teresa was back in control. She had taken her opponent's best shot, yet even while wobbled, had managed to toss off a macho smile to the corner. "We all know that Darwin holds back nothing. He's publicly confessed every wretched detail of his life. He's got nothing to lose. Let's ask him. Darwin, have you ever known me carnally?" She was supremely confident. What she did not know was that emotional turmoil now raged within Darwin Hunter. His gut spun like the rear wheels of a Pontiac in a snowy ditch, but his face was placid.

"No."

The forthrightness surprised even him. The denial rang like a bell across the audience, the bell that counted out Mimi Cox for a count of ten. His was even the accent of moral indignation. Further questions were irrelevant, and the murmuring crowd dispersed. Teresa came to the podium and gave him the same warm hand squeeze as after his Total Disclosure speech.

"I . . . I lied," stammered Darwin, now shaking.

"Of course you lied," purred Teresa. "That's why you're such a great politician. What I love about you is that there is such depth to your deception."

The following Monday was Labor Day. It was drizzling at race time, with promises of sunshine later in the day. Hannah and Tina had done an admirable job of reconciling the community, but only a hardy few cheered the runners off. There were ten contestants, a lead pack of five, an ex-contender (Darwin), and four others along for the ride.

Darwin looked forward to the pain he would inflict on himself in the race. He had been tormented since his on-stage lie the previous week. There was a major difference from his sin of omission, as far as Teresa was concerned, and his outright denial. For the first time in his adult life he did not know what to do next. He could see nothing but harm coming from an admission of his lie, and yet he could not continue with a campaign that had at its soul the honesty of its leader. He resolved to tell all to his campaign manager later that afternoon. Surely Captain Goo-Roo could summon some ancient rock-and-roll song words of comfort and wisdom.

Darwin reunited briefly with Sammi just before the race. He had seen her only in exchanges of cars, children, and mail for the past two months. She drove up alone just before the starting gun. He ran over, helped her out of the Saab and stood silently, holding both of her hands and gazing deeply into her eyes: What to say? Should he tell her how great she looked, or how much he missed her?

"Sammi." He spoke her name tenderly.

"Darwin."

"Sammi. I am so glad to see you." Don't be afraid to be vulnerable, he reminded himself.

"And I am so glad to see you." She mirrored his emphasis on *so*. She continued, "Because I've been trying to remember the name of that mechanic in Barre who does such a good job with imported cars. It's been driving me crazy! What is his name?"

The tenderness drained from his voice. "Eddie," he mumbled, "Eddie Tropiano."

"What did you say? Eddie Tropiano! I knew it was Italian, Tropiano. You don't know how much that's been bothering me."

"Always glad to be of service," Darwin's wrinkled smile returned, "ma'am."

At the half-mile mark Darwin had already dropped a hundred yards behind the leaders, although the rest of the also-rans trailed him by an equal amount. The drizzle had lightened and the sun was trying to break through, turning the air thick and comfortable. Comfortable, that is, unless you were trying to drag your carcass over eight hilly miles.

The Running of the Valley was a watershed for all participants, but especially for Darwin, the only person remaining who had run each one. Isn't it strange, he mused, how the hills never change, but people go through the wildest contortions imaginable? He thought back to the first running. They were hippies then, just glimpsing middle age over a distant horizon. Now, who knew what future wonders might unfold?

One unfolded at just that moment, in the form of a renegade runner sprinting onto the course from behind a tree. The runner was a man, shorter than Darwin, with the barrel chest of someone who worked for a living. He was wearing a ribbed undershirt, cut-off dress pants, and a pair of black, hightop U.S. Keds that showed the accumulated dust of twenty years in the closet.

Bennett. Bennett Blanchard.

Darwin was too shocked to speak. Here, running beside him, was the world's most unlikely jogger, a man who for years had ridiculed the pursuit as physical therapy for atrophied Flatlanders. Bennett was muttering as he ran:

"Whip your flat ass, I'm gonna. Beat you at your own game."

"Bennett, what's this all about?"

"It's about whipping your ass."

"Why?"

"You know why."

And Darwin did know why, he just thought it would be polite to ask. Bennett sprinted ahead ten yards, flapping noisily in his Keds. Darwin stayed discreetly behind, although he could hear Bennett exhorting himself. Within a mile they came to the first major hill. Bennett was already breathing heavily and his stride had lost all spring. Darwin eased alongside.

"You know, you have to train for this."

"Gonna grind you into this road," said Bennett, straight ahead, now heavily flushed with exertion. At the top of the first hill Bennett was practically running in place. Darwin slowed along with him. The nonstop stream of rhetoric had not ceased however.

"Bennett," said Darwin, "determination is not going to substitute for conditioning. You can hurt yourself by exerting yourself too much."

Bennett chugged on. All other runners were now out of sight, and the two men shared the canopied dirt road with only the forest and the birds.

"Let's stop and talk about it."

"I'm not stopping until you give up," he gasped. Another long hill stretched before them. Midway up, Bennett started retching. He drove to the top, then vomited. He tried to start again, but his innards would not let him. Darwin sprinted ahead to a water station set out earlier and came back with a cup for Bennett.

"Drink it. You'll be losing lots of fluids before this is over."

Bennett was doubled over, racked with convulsions. Darwin stood awkwardly, one hand holding a cup of water, the other resting lightly on Bennett's back. Finally, the last of the bile had been spit onto the road:

"First my wife, then my father, and now you see me puke all over my shoes."

Darwin handed him the cup. "Bennett, I'm not trying to steal your wife, or your father."

"There ever been anything between you'n her?"

"No."

You did it again! Darwin screamed at himself in mental disbelief at his own smooth treachery, then gritted his teeth, waiting for the lightning bolt. Instead he saw only the soft shaking of Bennett's head. Darwin spoke softly, although within him those same bald tires whined to free him from the ditch. "Teresa is completely true to you, Bennett."

"Then why is she working so hard for you?" The relief on Bennett's face was obvious. It made Darwin feel a little better.

"Damned if I know. C'mon. We've got to finish this course."

The two men started a slow lope. They alternately jogged and walked the remainder of the race. Bennett talked more to Darwin in that hour than he had to anyone in the previous decade. Insecurities spilled over like sap at the first boil, about Teresa, about the future of the farm and his ability to keep it together for his son, Olin.

"It'll be there," said Darwin reassuringly. "If anyone can keep it together, you can."

A half mile before the finish Darwin suggested they pick up the pace. "No," said Bennett. "Since I'm not going to whip your ass, I'd justa soon no one even knew I ran. I'll just cut through the woods back to the house."

"Okay," said Darwin, "but will you come to the cook-out?"

"I've gotta million things to do," said Bennett, "but I suppose I can drop by for a minute. See you there."

Darwin crossed the line with his slowest time ever. The sun had baked through the drizzle. Billy Mann had tapped the keg. The kids were scattering from Sunny like minnows from a tuna. Howard "Warren" Pease was expounding to a semi-interested Gimp Fenvessey on the rise and fall of the fitness movement, relating it directly to the Bicentennial. Stella Blanchard turned the folding tables into a potluck panorama. Hoyt was bouncing his grandson Olin on his knee. Sammi and Martha Gunion were catching up on a summer's worth of gossip. The town was battered, but intact. Only Sue Clarke was missing. Incensed at her husband beyond communication, she was visiting the Celtics training camp, the guest of Slinging Stevie Mugford. Townshend appeared with a hangdog expression, actually much closer to what everyone knew as the real thing than the shaved entrepreneur of recent vintage. He kept his daughter Heather, arm in sling, by his side.

Darwin sought out the winner, the doelike Tina Pisano, for congratulations.

"Admit it," she said, laughing. "The better man won."

" 'Victory is Birth, without sight or sense, neither man nor woman. Pure beginning.' "

Tina was disarmed by the heartfelt tone and supplemented Darwin's handshake with a sweaty hug. "That's really nice, Darwin. Where's it from?"

"The preface to my autobiography, *Welcome to My Dinkdom*. Seriously—great job!" He left Tina in order to seek out his campaign manager.

"Captain, I've got to talk to you," Darwin said. "I couldn't sleep at all last night."

Billy Mann could hear the urgency in Darwin's voice. He was sitting cross-legged, fiddling with his acoustic guitar, performing for anyone who stopped by.

"Reminds me of a tune," he murmured. "Shoot."

"Not now, but after everyone leaves. It's important!"

"How did I guess? Don't you worry, darling, I'll be there."

If one squinted just a little, time was reversed and the players of *Beyond Yonder* were celebrating yet another communal gathering of the hip and the hick, Flatlanders and Chucks on neutral turf.

Darwin tried to be his most attentive to Sammi, but he was careful to maintain distance as well. She seemed more interested in catching up with neighbors than talking with him. He tried hard not to be offended.

He was able to rustle up a fairly lively horseshoe round robin. Bennett and Emil dominated, although the team of Joe Pisano and Sunny Moss extended them to the max. Darwin made a few foot-foul jokes that brought to mind the Stowe Stallion. Warren Pease took on B. J. Bosco's former role as rules official. As always, his knowledge was as encyclopedic as his delivery turgid. Darwin told Joe if the lecture was titled, it would be called, "Ten Times More than You Ever Cared to Know about Horseshoes."

But the game prevailed, shoes clanking a rhythm that led an afternoon on to its appropriate conclusion. The harmony was best expressed by Emil Dummerston Weed, who celebrated a ringer with a long draft from a fresh cup of beer, then exclaimed, "Horseshoes without beer is like a kiss without tongue."

The men guffawed. Sunny's cheeks turned a bright red and she gently reprimanded Emil, "Aw, shut up, Dummy."

Emil's smile, yellowed and wattled, gleamed nonetheless. "Is that any way," he asked, "for the girl I'm going to marry to be talkin'?" There was a collective held breath, followed by an outpouring of handshakes, congratulations, and fresh beers all around.

By late afternoon the Running of the Valley was history. The kids rooted around like truffle-seeking pigs for deposit bottles, while the Captain and Darwin walked in tandem from point to point with their Hefty trash bags.

"Billy, I've lied to you. I've lied to everyone." The response was silence. The stage was Darwin's. He told of a Tunbridge Fair, years earlier, when a chance meeting with Teresa Blanchard turned into repeated visits to the beer hall and culminated with unbridled passion in the passenger seat of the Saab. Now the lie, not the act, had become the greater of the sins. Billy's silence commanded him to continue, and Darwin portrayed a disjointed tale of marital strife, seductive advances from a political rival, and his recent perpetuation of the falsehood first in public, then private. Darwin envisioned his mouth as the opening of an aerosol can. When he finished, the two men continued collecting the flotsam and jetsam of the celebration in neat, green bags. The Captain spoke when the last bag was twisted shut:

"If you're waiting for me to judge you, you'll wait a long time. I'm your campaign manager. My job is to get you elected, just as a doctor's is to cure you or a lawyer's to protect you."

"But how can you believe in me?"

"I believe in you. Reminds me of a tune. You are a mortal human, capable of lying, self-deception, and occasional piss-poor judgment. The question is, what do you want to do now?"

"I . . . I don't know. It's like I start thinking about what to do, and my brain shuts down. I feel like I could freeze right here in this position for the rest of my life."

"I've been there," said Billy. He even permitted himself a little laugh. "Let me tell you my life story sometime." He shook away a mindful of memories.

"As your campaign manager I see three possibilities. First, you could dummy up and say nothing. Teresa won't say anything. I won't say anything. No one else knows. Second, you could drop from the race. Just avoid the issue. Or finally, you could tell everything as an extension of Total Disclosure."

"That would be terrific," said Darwin. "We'd have at least two murders, a suicide, and a public lynching."

"I see it going one of two ways," said the Captain, his mind projecting into the future. "Either you'd get crucified, or people would forgive you and say that Total Disclosure really did have validity."

"My money is on crucifixion."

The men sat at the picnic table, the last of the summer fading behind the hills and the last of the keg swishing in their bellies. Finally, it was Darwin who summarized:

"I give up. What do we do?"

"No," said Billy, "what do *you* do? I don't make this decision. I help you make the best decision. That's my role."

Darwin nodded. Billy was right. "I don't know what to do."

"What would help?"

Darwin shook his head. "I seem to be incapable of making this decision."

The Captain nudged him along, as would a tugboat: "Would it help to talk to someone?"

"That's what I'm trying to accomplish with you, but you keep pushing the responsibility back onto me."

"Someone else maybe? Sammi?"

Darwin shook his head.

"Teresa?"

More shakes, more emphatic.

"Any friends?"

The suggestion checked the side sweeps of Darwin's head. "Yes," he said enthusiastically. "That's it. B.J. and the Stallion. They know me from a time when life was simpler. I'll call them." The Captain nodded encouragement, and for the first time that afternoon Darwin began accumulating momentum:

"B.J. and the Stallion lived here. They know me, they

know the players, they know the area. They're definitely the ones I need."

"Do you trust their judgment?"

"Hell, no," said Darwin. "They're two of the more unbalanced personalities I have ever known. But what I need is perspective, and these guys can give you more perspective than Carter has little liver pills."

"Nice image."

"Yeah, they've got perspective up the wazoo. You're right. I don't need people to make my decisions, but rather, people who can push me off dead center."

"Now we're cooking. But one problem. Real communication cannot take place over a telephone wire. You're going to have to see them in person."

"That's impossible. The Stallion's in Manhattan someplace. And B.J.'s in Florida."

The Captain shrugged. His gesture said there was no problem. "My only commitment is to be back by next Sunday. Can't miss a date at the Club 100. How soon can you be ready?"

Darwin needed only a second of looking at Billy to realize that he was serious. "I dunno. This really is pretty crazy. The kids start school this week. I know Sunny can handle that, but I've got a shitload of patients scheduled. Of course, I can arrange to lay them off on someone, but I also had some campaign things lined up. I like the idea of going to see these people and getting my head straightened around, but I'm not sure if just packing up and flying off to New York and Florida is possible this week." Darwin looked at Billy and felt his objections wilt.

"Who said anything about flying? We're driving, white man."

12

Beyond Beyond

They left that night, inspiration, not logic, their guiding star. Captain Goo-Roo had little green pills that sustained him through the night. He would not share them with Darwin, commanding him, instead, to sleep. The Captain, meanwhile, sang an extensive set of songs having to do with New York or the city. Darwin slept fitfully, waking every few minutes as the driver launched into another song. "On Broadway" led to "Summer in the City" which led to "New York, New York" which led to the entire musical score to *West Side Story*. The cities ticked by— Rutland, Glens Falls, Albany, Poughkeepsie, Peekskill. They descended the paved Hudson, arriving in Manhattan at five A.M.

"Great planning," mused Darwin as they cruised the blue-lit streets. "We made such great time, we can hang around for half the day." They ate breakfast, scrambled eggs and Schaefer beer, alongside stevedores at the Fulton Fish Market. These men were just finishing their day's work. Darwin's had just begun.

189

Locating the Stallion was the first chore. Darwin's news of Bruce Liebermann had been scant since he left Upper Granville. He tried directory assistance, but, of course, the number was unlisted. He knew that his friend was still in the restoration business, transferring his mantle of architectural superiority from the Northwoods to the paved streets, but beyond that he had no clue as to his whereabouts. Working out of a phone booth in Grand Central Station, Darwin tracked down the Stallion's brother, a Manhattan attorney, and got the name of the business and a phone number. Darwin called three times, but Bruce was either "on another line," "with a client," or "in a meeting." Finally Darwin left a message that he was on his way, with an entreaty for Bruce to please make time for him.

"Doesn't sound like the guy really wants to see you," said Billy.

"Well, you have to understand Bruce. He thinks things like enthusiasm and sentiment are bad for his image. Plus, of all the most important men in the world, he is the most important. Beneath the veneer, however—"

"Is plywood," interjected Captain Goo-Roo.

"Don't ask me to explain the Stowe Stallion. He's a remarkable person, and he's my friend," Darwin sniffed defensively.

The showroom for American Excess was located in an old brick warehouse not far from the entrance to the Holland Tunnel. The sign, gold letters on a black background, identified SPECIALISTS IN ARCHITECTURAL DETAIL, alerting one about what to expect inside: a cavernous space filled with random bits of our architectural past—windows, columns, door frames, back bars, mantels, moldings. The display is strictly functional, although carefully aimed spotlighting highlights the merchandise.

There were no prices, but rather, hang tags filled out with blunt pencil markings, which provided tantalizing glimpses into history: 1855; cast by Glenwood, Troy, N.Y.; original milk paint. The floor bustled with goods moving in and out. A complete banister was wheeled in on a dolly; a forklift ferried pallets loaded with stamped tin ceilings. The staff had bright eyes and dirty hands. Questions? They'd stop and talk. Prices? Hey, see the lady at the counter.

In the center of the tasteful ruin was a horseshoe-shaped counter, itself a relic from a turn-of-the-century shoe factory. It was for sale too. The woman within the horseshoe was black and casual. Blue jeans and a work shirt could not hide her spectacular beauty. Her hands were clean.

Some fine print on the sign outside provided another clue as to what to expect inside. NATHANIEL HALE WINTHROP, PROPRIETOR. Darwin remembered it as the nom de plane that the Stallion used in Vermont as well.

"Is Bruce Liebermann here?" asked Darwin. He was alone, Captain Goo-Roo opting for sleep and not wanting to be a third party to this small reunion.

"Are you Darwin?" He nodded. She smiled and continued, "There is no Bruce here. There is a Nathaniel, however. He has this theory that people won't buy Americana from a Jew."

"It's encouraging to know that some things never change—except little things like names and places."

"Were you a client?"

Darwin laughed. "No, I was a friend and neighbor."

"I've known Nat to have clients and neighbors," said the woman with a smile, "but he's not real big in the friend department."

"Well, I'm a friend, loyal, true, and eternal." Darwin

was so taken by the young lady that he took a chance: "And my life is in shambles at the present, and I've come to Bruce—er, Nat—for advice."

"The words Nat and advice aren't generally used in the same sentence unless the word bad is in there too. You're going to have to wait for your advice. He's on a job right now. Back in an hour. He told me to entertain you."

"Know any good jokes?"

"Yeah. You hear the one about the guy who drove from Vermont to get advice from Nathaniel Hale Winthrop?"

Darwin really liked this girl. "How well do you know him?"

"We're living together." The Stowe Stallion's taste, thought Darwin, was as impeccable in women as it was in architecture.

When Bruce Liebermann arrived two hours later, he had Captain Goo-Roo in tow. "Who's your friend?" he said to Darwin.

"Bruce, this is Billy Mann."

"Captain Goo-Roo?" Bruce showed surprise along with recognition. "I knew you looked familiar. I've seen you perform. You're an institution."

"My fame has obviously spread south."

Bruce addressed Darwin first: "Yeah, to Rutland. I saw the van with Vermont plates outside and thought it was you sleeping inside. So I shake this dude out of slumber city. Hey Captain, if you're interested in doing some gigs in the city, I've got some people I could talk to. We did the interior of this club downtown, a real Louis the Fifteenth trip, where they would love you."

Bruce Liebermann had not, to Darwin's eyes, aged, except for some deepened character lines around the eyes.

His shock of black curly hair was shorter than he wore it in Vermont, with just the slightest aurora of silver.

"You're looking good for an old man," said Darwin.

"Yeah, right," said the Stallion.

"But I can still beat your butt around the valley." Darwin knew that a competitive challenge was as irresistible to the Stallion as sugar lumps.

Not this time, however, as he got a second, "Yeah, right" in response.

"Can we talk?" asked Darwin.

"If you want," replied Bruce, "but I have lots of things to do." His lack of apparent interest was overwhelming.

Darwin, Bruce, the Captain, and the black girl, Pam, crowded into the small private space of Nathaniel Hale Winthrop's office. He sat behind a massive desk that had once been a table for folding linens in a textile factory; the others sat in wooden chairs of diverse, but equally meaningful origin. Darwin told his story in just over half an hour. Bruce was not completely unfamiliar with the situation, having seen some of the national press coverage accorded Total Disclosure. He showed an occasional flicker of recognition, but otherwise no emotion. There was no shared pain at Darwin and Sammi's separation, no mirth at Bennett Blanchard clopping along in the Running of the Valley, no surprise at the Tunbridge Fair liaison of a farmer's wife and an opthalmologist.

Darwin's verbal stream meandered to his present situation, caught in a trap that had not injured him but had left him paralyzed. "I want to do the right thing," he said in summary, "but I have no idea what that is. That's why I'm here. You know me as well as anyone. I'd like you to help."

The Stallion had been fiddling with an antique wooden plane. He actually shaved little bits off his desk during Darwin's monologue, tinkered with adjustments, then tried again. Occasionally he grabbed a fly swatter and took a violent whack at an unsuspecting insect. When he realized that the burden of conversation was upon him, he spoke slowly, without removing his gaze from his tool or his prey:

"You may have no idea what the right thing to do is, but I don't care what it is."

Darwin immediately protested: "You may not care about who wins the election, but you care about the people. We lived in this intense little world for eight years. We shared everything from bottles of wine to each others' wives. We ran a thousand miles together in sleet, mud, and snow. We've gotten drunk and stoned. We've shared a big slice of lifetime. You've got to care." Darwin meant the last statement as an awakening slap.

The Stowe Stallion resisted the stimulation with a wall of ennui. "I'm not insensitive, but I don't care. I don't give a shit if Townshend Clarke cuts his head off, let alone shaves it. I don't care if Walt Gunion lines the valley with skyscrapers. They're not people to me anymore. They're not part of my life. They're abstractions of my memory."

"What about me?" Darwin was erect in his chair, remembering the support he had provided Bruce in some of the lower moments of his life. "Do you care about me?"

"No." The Stallion looked through him, not with aggression, not with pain, not with ice water in his veins, but rather Novocain. "Believe me. I just don't care." If Darwin had picked a word to describe Bruce's tone, it would have been *sincere*. He excused himself, saying that he was keeping a client waiting.

Suddenly he was gone. There was silence, then soft sobbing from Pam. Her feelings came bubbling to the surface the moment Darwin touched her shoulder to comfort her:

"I don't know what he's feeling. He works and works, and pushes and drives. He never shares anything from his past! He says he loves me, but it means the same as when he says he loves travertine marble."

"There's a person under there someplace," said Darwin, realizing that it had been a mistake to have Pam present at the meeting.

"Yeah," chimed in the Captain. "He's just been buried by an avalanche. Let's go, my friend. We're on a time-table."

The van pointed south. Darwin babbled from Manhattan to the Delaware Memorial Bridge. The visit had been most worthwhile, he claimed. Talk about perspective! His vision was broadened magnificently from the Stallion's change of life and change of heart. He admitted, however, that he was not an inch closer to understanding himself and what had to be done. B.J. would be different, he assured the Captain. B.J. would be completely different.

The travelers stopped in Pikesville, Maryland, just west of Baltimore, for a steaming platter of Chesapeake Bay crabs and pitchers of beer. It was eleven o'clock when they finished smashing and slurping. It was the most therapeutic meal of Darwin's life. "Now," he said, wiping the last of the crustacean detritus from his chin, "for a sleazy motel."

"No way," said Captain Goo-Roo. "I've got to be back for Sunday. We're driving. Why do you think I brought these little green pills?" When Darwin awoke, Maryland, Virginia, and most of North Carolina had been turned under their burning rubber. The Captain was humming away at his next Sunday-night extravaganza. Darwin had never realized the hours of skill-honing necessary to present a seemingly spontaneous show to such a small audience.

"Why do you do it?" asked Darwin.

"Because I'm an artist, and an artist is like a heroin addict. He can't help himself." Darwin believed him.

Breakfast was grits and biscuits at a truck stop. Lunch was peaches and boiled Georgia peanuts from a roadside stand. At dusk they crossed the Florida border, an accomplishment of enough significance to warrant a rousing cheer.

"Okay," said the Captain. "Now, where in Florida is she?"

"Someplace called Muscle Bayou. It's near Pensacola, I think."

"Pensacola? That's on the other side of the state!"

"Isn't it near Fort Lauderdale?"

A visitor's welcome center loomed before them. Billy screeched on the brakes and drove in. "Darwin, we can either go ten hours south or ten hours west or anywhere in between, but the time to decide is now. I'm going to sleep. You better get your shit together."

While the Captain crashed into dreamland, Darwin logged time with the pay phone and road maps. Finally he pieced it together. B.J., who hailed originally from Fort Lauderdale, was now the proprietress of a modest establishment bearing her name in the town of Muscle Bayou on the Gulf Coast. The place even had a phone listing and a person who answered Darwin's call. B.J., he learned, was out on her shrimp boat. Darwin left word that he was on his way, and got his rudimentary directions. A shrimp boat. This was an unexpected development, but unexpected developments were the norm for persons of voracious appetites like B.J. He tried to rouse the Captain to give him news of his success, but elicited only muffled grunts.

Darwin fumbled his way westward through the night, arriving in the general environs of Muscle Bayou at two A.M. Darwin's mind had clouded over by this time. Billy was still dead asleep. So Darwin parked the van at a spot overlooking the Gulf of Mexico. B.J. would wait until the morning.

Darwin awoke to the sound of sea gulls. He checked his watch. Six A.M. The Captain had been asleep for twelve hours. It was the dawn of a spectacular day, the southern air thick with humidity and fetid vegetation. He started the van and found a roadside diner where they received biscuits with red-eye gravy and directions.

B.J.'s Riviera Room was located on the end of a pier in the tiny fishing port of Muscle Bayou. It was a weathered shack with a tin roof enclosing a tiny bar, a pinball machine, a small kitchen, and a few tables and chairs. It opened onto a deck with worn cleats where the shrimp boats tied up each night.

"You Darwin?" asked the man behind the bar when the northern travelers arrived at seven-thirty A.M. He was a leathered man about thirty-five or fifty-five, wearing the flamboyant straw cowboy hat so favored by Riviera Rednecks.

"I'm Darwin."

"You jist 'bout mist 'er. Better hustle yer buns onto the boat." He tilted his hat in the direction of a lubdubbing diesel clearing its throat.

Darwin and the Captain obeyed, bursting from the lounge into the daylight and directly into B.J.'s blond hair and ample bosom.

"You're late," she boomed at Darwin. "Whose yer friend?" Then she bear hugged Darwin so hard he thought his head might pop off, but he squeezed back just as hard. Thirty seconds later they were chugging out into the calm waters of the Gulf of Mexico.

There was little time for catching up on the boat. B.J. told Darwin that her father had died and left her a tidy sum of money. She had been en route to Vermont (on a motorcycle) when she met a shrimper in a bar. Before long she was working the nets out in the Gulf, and when the Riviera Room became available, she could not resist.

B.J. was definitely the captain of this ship. There was a Tugboat Annie quality to her, but at the same time Darwin had never seen her so tanned and fit. Occasionally she would pull out her thirty-five millimeter camera, and Darwin remembered that her Radcliffe education had prepared her for more than running a redneck bar and shrimp boat. She barked commands and men scurried. It was a frantic day, but mercifully short. By three in the afternoon the shrimp had been iced down and sold, the nets put up, and the decks hosed down.

Darwin and Billy went to B.J.'s modest abode and scoured the accumulated road grime, salt, and shrimp scales before going back to the Riviera Room for some serious catching up. B.J. was waiting for them on the deck with a galvanized tub of ice, oysters, and beer. The sun slipped into the placid Gulf as easily as dozens of oysters slid down the throats of the threesome. B.J. learned that Billy was a musician, and soon there was a guitar at his disposal.

"You'd like it down here," she assured Darwin. "We work hard, play harder, go to bed early, and then do it again." Eventually there was a lull. B.J. took a sip of beer and changed the course of the conversation. "So what brings you to Muscle Bayou, Darwin?"

She proved the antithesis of the Stallion as an audience. She guffawed at the transformation of Townshend; she sighed at the plight of Darwin and Sammi; she roared at Total Disclosure; she snickered at Riley Gore; she cried when she heard of Hoyt Blanchard's heart attack. She pressed for more details, making Darwin repeat certain passages over and over. She was suitably dumbfounded by Darwin's revelations about Teresa, and fully sympathetic with the tangled web in which life had enveloped her friend.

"Did you notice the name of my boat?" she asked suddenly. Neither man had. "Don't miss it tomorrow morning," she commanded. Darwin and Billy had already decided that they could tarry no longer. In the morning they would be northward bound.

"So what do I do, B.J.?" asked Darwin.

"I dunno, go to bed, I guess," she said. Then, looking directly at Billy Mann: "You coming?"

"You've got to help me," protested Darwin.

"Okay, I'll help. Um, divorce Sammi, marry Teresa, screw the election, and move down here. No, don't marry Teresa and move down here; divorce Sammi, marry Weinstein, win the election, and don't move down here. No, marry Sue Clarke, commit yourself, and live in the mental institute. No—"

"This isn't helping me," said Darwin.

B.J. smiled. "Darwin, you're a big boy. You can't believe that I have pearls of wisdom ready to dispense in situations like these. Whatever you do is going to be right, believe me. I trust your judgment. You're as honest a man as there is in the world. Just make sure to check out the name of my boat in the morning. It'll blow your mind."

The conversation had come to its natural end.

"Let's go to bed," said B.J. with finality. "Wake-up call is five A.M. They make up breakfasts here that are unbelievable. I've got a soft couch for you, Darwin. Meanwhile I'm going to teach your friend a few things about safe sex."

Darwin slept soundly, dreaming of shrimp boats and soft nights. B.J. roused him at five. Captain Goo-Roo wore a look of beatific bliss. "Reminds me of a tune, a very long, energetic, raunchy tune," he said.

Back at the Riviera Room they chowed down omelets smothered with shrimp gravy, biscuits, grits, and coffee. B.J. kissed them both on the lips and cast off the bow line herself. "Just watch my back," she said. So they did, smiling when the exposed fantail revealed the craft's name, DARWIN'S DILEMMA. Both men stood smiling as the lubdub faded by the second, both feeling that three thousand miles was a small effort to justify this experience.

Billy Mann jolted the van into gear, and they were homeward bound. Neither man spoke; Billy did not even sing. Finally, crossing the Georgia line, Darwin turned on the radio. It barely crackled to life before Billy snapped:

"Why in the world did you do that?"

"Thought we could listen to some music."

Billy clicked it off. "If it's music you want, we can make it."

"I'm sorry. Sing me some songs about the sea."

Billy responded with a haunting set of seafaring ballads, drawn from simpler times. There was no rock and roll here, just stories of men who left the land on boats. The men were Norwegian, Polish, Irish, and Canadian. They worked the waters of Lake Michigan, the Baltic, the Solway Firth, the Bay of Fundy. They sang about whiskey and women, women and whiskey. They told tales of cruel captains, brave captains, cowardly captains; of storms that snapped or inhaled ships, of nefarious hidden reefs, of being adrift and lost. Of women remembered.

Darwin indulged himself for—how long?—three hours? There was air-conditioning in the van, but both preferred to blast onward with the windows open. Darwin was as close to nude as possible—bare feet, nylon running shorts, and a white cotton tank top—while Billy maintained the dignity of a tee-shirt, faded jeans, and cowboy boots. Conversation was largely superfluous, although at the end of the marathon set of sea tunes, Darwin said:

"How do you know all those songs?"

"Oh, just picked'em up from the radio."

"I mean, really."

"Hey! This is your Captain. Captains sail the seas. There was saltwater in my blood before there was rock and roll." And with that came Captain Goo-Roo's life story, a saga that began simultaneously in 1948 and North Georgia. There was a father—a career Navy man and an alcoholic —a suffering mother, and saltwater. Just those three elements took up four hours of the trip north.

It was the Captain's description of his summers spent as a professional clammer on Narragansett Bay that gave Darwin a sudden inspiration.

"How long would it take us to detour to New Bedford?"

"New Bedford, that's almost to Cape Cod."

"Close enough."

"About eight hours."

"Can you afford the time?"

"I told you, as long as I'm back on Sunday night, I'm golden."

"Let's do it, then. I've just figured what's going to pull everything into focus for me."

Twenty-five hours of straight driving brought Darwin Hunter and Billy Mann to a Texaco station just off of Interstate 195 in New Bedford. Darwin checked out the phone book and struck instant pay dirt; an M. Gomes was listed on Periwinkle Way. He dialed the number and, on the third ring, a female voice answered. Darwin's speech was already prepared:

"Is this Rosa Marquita Gomes?"

"Yes."

"Mrs. Gomes—am I pronouncing your name right?—Mrs. Gomes, my name is Darwin Hunter and I'm a friend of Hoyt Blanchard's in Vermont."

"A friend of Hoyt's? Is Hoyt . . . is Hoyt all right?"

"Yes, he is, Mrs. Gomes. Would it be possible to come by to see you?"

"Did Hoyt send you?"

"No, ma'am. But he told me about you, and I wanted to meet you."

"Yes, you can come by. When would that be?"

"I'm in New Bedford now. Could you do it soon?"

"I'll put on some tea."

Rosa Marquita Gomes's white clapboard house on Periwinkle Way was as neat as Stella Blanchard's perennial garden. The street was small, shaded, and old, an architectural hodgepodge that started in the 1850s with Rosa's half Cape and continued through the 1950s, when the last lot was filled with a crackerbox made in a factory that was painted, in succession, pink, lime, avocado, and harvest gold.

Rosa's husband, Caitano, bought the house in 1928, then

in complete disrepair. The time in between trips to sea was spent in loving reconstruction, and the job was complete when Caitano's boat encountered a fifty-foot rogue wave in the Grand Banks. Nine Portagees perished, an event of such significance that the *Boston Globe* devoted an entire paragraph to it three weeks after they were officially declared missing. There were no survivors.

The Portuguese community supported its own as best it could. Caitano had been diligent, as well as ineligible for credit, and had purchased his house for cash. Rosa was left without debt or hope. She was twenty-four years old.

Darwin knocked on the door. He was alone. Billy insisted that his presence would be a needless threat, and slept in the van, looking forward to Darwin's eventual narration of the meeting.

Rosa Marquita, by Darwin's estimation, looked fifteen years younger than Hoyt Blanchard. Some of the difference was the swarthiness of her skin, some the blessings of her sex. The rest was pure magic.

She invited Darwin in. In the parlor there was a baby grand piano, the top of which was covered by propped-up photographs, standing tall and proud like the tents of soldiers on bivouac. She noticed Darwin scanning the pictures and accommodated his curiosity:

"That's my son, Caitano. He was named after my first husband. These are my three grandchildren, Stephen—he's going to be a lawyer like his father—Donna, a sophomore at Massachusetts Community College, and Michael—he's a junior in high school and plays in one of those rock and roll bands. This is my second husband, Jesus, whom we all called Pepe. He died, it will be fifteen years this November. We were married forty-three years."

She paused, although there were more photographs to

describe, reminding herself that this was a stranger in her house. Darwin took the cue:

"I'm not here with any message, Mrs. Gomes. I came completely on my own. Hoyt told me about you. I'm the only person he has ever told. He's getting old, Mrs. Gomes. He's had a heart attack, and I thought when I went back to Vermont he would be comforted by news that you were all right."

Darwin watched her brown eyes for a sign. They were friendly, but with a depth and distance that he could not interpret.

"There's one more picture," was all she said.

She went to the bottom drawer of a bedside table, and from under some clothes withdrew a small pink plastic bag with a drawstring. She came back out to the parlor and sat on the couch. Darwin joined her as she opened the bag as gently as if it contained a child's dreams. There was one blurry photograph, taken at an amusement park, of a young man with dark hair and square shoulders, his arm around a woman who fit perfectly beside him. The faces were shaded, but Darwin recognized them as dear friends. There were scraps of paper—a pay stub, a grocery list, a tender note written in a rough hand.

Rosa got up, went into the kitchen, and returned with a blue willow tea service. There were slices of Portuguese sweet bread, a pot of orange marmalade, sliced lemons arranged on a saucer, a pitcher of milk, and a bowl of sugar cubes with silver tongs for serving. She did not ask Darwin if he wanted tea, but went ahead and poured.

"You may drink from Hoyt's cup," she said with a smile. "We bought this set as a Christmas present to ourselves, the only Christmas we ever spent together. Here's the receipt." She rummaged through the pile of scraps to show Darwin.

"Some of the happiest times of my life were spent sipping tea with Hoyt and this tea set.

"The summer I met Hoyt, we were two of the loneliest people on this earth. I'd lost my Caitano just a year before, and for Hoyt it was the first time that the farm had ever gone on without him. We came together so quick and natural that neither of us knew what hit us. Before I knew it, the sweetest boy in the world was lying next to me, and suddenly I felt like living again. We had close to two years together, but it was a lifetime for me."

"Why didn't you marry him?" Darwin asked the question tentatively, knowing that he was entering territory where he had no right to tread. To his surprise, Rosa brightened and laughed.

"Can you imagine that! Hoyt comes back to his little town from the big city with a dark-skinned girl. What would the schoolteacher think? What about his parents and brothers and sisters? They'd turn him away from that place as sure as we're sitting here. I couldn't have lived there, no more than he could have lived here. Oh, I loved that boy, but we were not meant to be. Did he marry that school lady?"

Oh yes, said Darwin, and described a life of sharing, love, and struggle on a Vermont dairy farm. Good, good, murmured Rosa Marquita Gomes as Darwin told her about their children, the town of Upper Granville and its contentious array of characters. More tea was served, and the marmalade spooned onto the sweet bread, as Darwin carried on about cold winters, whole-herd buyout programs, Christmas services in the community church, John Deere tractors, and all those things that made up the world of Hoyt Blanchard. It was a very happy life that Darwin portrayed, and it gave immense pleasure to an old lady with brown pools for eyes.

205

The sun shone through dainty curtains into the house on Periwinkle Way, just as Hoyt had described it to Darwin. Time and tea slipped away. Darwin was told about a separate, but equally happy life, spent with a gentleman called Pepe who played guitar and made his own vinho verde, a man who in later years took her to Florida each winter and who took her on a return visit to the Cape Verde Islands for her seventieth birthday. He heard about a son, now almost ready to retire, who became a lawyer and city councilman, attending the 1960 Democratic Convention as a delegate for John F. Kennedy. He heard about grandchildren, and was shown more pictures.

It was easy time, passed with someone with whom Darwin felt instant kinship. A natural ending came, and Darwin asked the question he had been avoiding: was Hoyt's perception of Rosa's pregnancy at the time of their departure accurate?

"I lost that child," she said, without flinching, "very soon after Hoyt left. Pepe had just arrived from the old country and needed a woman to look after him. He didn't speak a word of English. I married him and became pregnant with Caitano right away. He was a very nice man, and worked hard for us." Her face, as calm as the sea at sunset, left no questions to be asked. Nor did the picture on the piano, a Latin version of Hoyt Blanchard. As Darwin shook Rosa's hand to leave, she had a last thought.

"Take this," she said, wiping out Darwin's tea cup with a napkin. "Hoyt would like this."

"But it breaks up the set," protested Darwin.

"Take it," she said happily. "You'll make an old man and an old woman very happy."

13

The World According to Tunbridge

"Hey, Gimp, what's the story?"

"Yeah, why'd you drag us out here?"

Gimp Fenvessey slouched at one of the long row tables in the Tunbridge Fair Beer Hall, a dank space beneath a grandstand that for two or three brief nights a year was the best place in Central Vermont, if not the world, to drink beer. This was not one of those times, however. It was ten A.M. on Friday morning of the one-hundred-twentieth Tunbridge World's Fair. The Central Vermont press corps, a scraggly band of eight men and five women, had been enticed to a mysterious press conference by Gimp Fenvessey.

"This will be worth it. You'll all get bylines and justification for your stringer fees. Plus you can put your fried dough and onion rings on the expense account." Gimp teased everyone with a long pause, then aimed his camera at Cilly Dupras, a freelancer for *People* and *The New York Times*, who answered with an expletive.

"C'mon, douche bag, grow up!" interjected Benny Malone, a photographer for the *Burlington Free Press*, and one-time resident of Upper Granville. "Does it have anything to do with Darwin and Total Disclosure?" Most of the present company had attended the Fools Fling and had seen the nation's curiosity piqued.

Another reporter snatched up Fenvessey's film bag. "Come clean, Gimp, or you'll never see these pictures alive again."

Gimp made a half-hearted swipe with his deformed arm. "Go ahead, take advantage of a cripple. You guys are just jealous because you can't use the handicapped parking spaces."

"Yeah, and those nice, roomy toilets," shot back Cilly. "What is it, Fenvessey?"

"Okay, okay, okay. Darwin Hunter called the press conference, and it does have to do with Total Disclosure, and that's all I know."

"I wonder if he's pulling out?"

Benny Malone laughed. "Knowing Darwin, when he talks about 'pulling out' he's talking about birth control, not politics."

"Maybe he has more to disclose?"

"Why is he doing this at the Tunbridge Fair?"

"I dunno," said Fenvessey with a shake of the head. "I have no goddamn idea."

Tunbridge, Vermont, is like a big Upper Granville, nestled comfortably in a valley bowl, surrounded by hardwoods and, beyond that, blue sky. The World's Fair has its roots deep in the state's agricultural traditions. Ox pulls compete with the honky-tonk of the midway to give the locals a final respite prior to the onset of winter. The Fair is held on the third weekend of September, a time that offers glorious days, nippy evenings, and usually rain on Saturday night. There is country music, rock and roll, junk food galore, a tiny dance hall, and just enough sleaze to make sure that all tastes are catered to. From the judging of zucchini to the late-night carousing in parking lots, the Tunbridge Fair satisfies the righteous, the rigorous, and the ridiculous.

The Fair also draws enough of a crowd that in election years it is a favorite stumping ground for local candidates. From the governor to the Darwins, all candidates pay homage to the common man by eating fried dough and pumping flesh at the fairgrounds.

"Just remember," said Gimp, loading his camera with one hand and clicking off a few film-advancing shots, "the last time Darwin Hunter called a press conference was one of the best shows of the year. His Total Disclosure announcement was carried everywhere, MacNeil/Lehrer, *People, Time, Newsweek, the Times*, the wire services, you name it.

"So now that he's exposed everything," asked one of the other six reporters on the scene, "what's left?"

"I'm not sure," said Gimp thoughtfully. "I've just known Darwin long enough that whatever he says is bound to be interesting. Except when he's had four or five beers, and the chances of that right now is only, say, two out of five."

"Hey, whatever happened to those other guys, the ones with the big plan for the colonial theme park?"

"Died a natural death," answered Gimp with a laugh. "A painful, protracted, agonizing, but natural, death."

"I heard something about a kid getting shot."

"Are you talking about the guy whose wife ran off with the basketball player?"

Billy Mann came out, made a beeline toward Gimp. "We all set?" he asked. Receiving Gimp's confirmation, he waved to the back and Darwin came forward. He wore jeans, a turtleneck, and a worn chamois shirt. He carried no notes. He walked to a table in front of Gimp and looked at him:

"What do I do now?"

"Do you have a statement?"

"Right, yes, I have a statement." Silence.

"Well, make the statement."

Darwin acted as if he suddenly understood the punchline. "Oh, right! I haven't done this before, can you guess? So here goes. My name is Darwin Hunter and I am a candidate for the State Senate representing the Fifth District of Vermont. I announced my candidacy last April, promising to follow a policy of Total Disclosure. I promised the people of Central Vermont that I would be completely open and completely honest. That has been the foundation of my entire campaign.

"It is my sad duty now to tell the people of Central Vermont that I am a complete liar. Not only did I not disclose a particular incident in my original announcement, but I have conspired to cover it up ever since. I have deceived people, I've lied, I'm sorry, I apologize. What can I say? I feel lower than whale shit.

"I have decided not to withdraw from the race, however. By seeing it through to conclusion the people of Central Vermont may use their vote to condemn me. I deserve it.

"That's the statement. Like I say, I'm kind of a Gary Hart, Jim and Tammy Faye, and Jimmy Swaggart rolled into one. Any questions?"

There were a total of fourteen reporters in the room, all of whom knew they were on the verge of the most juicy, gossipy scoop of their lives. They spoke as one, with the unity of the Mormon Tabernacle Choir:

"WHAT DID YOU DO?"

"Uh, Darwin, ah . . . Mr. Hunter," said Gimp, solo voce. "What was the lie?"

Darwin laughed. "Now do you believe I'm nervous? You've heard of Freudian slips? Well, this is a Freudian chasm. You're gonna love this. Here's my story, it's sad but true."

"Reminds me of a tune," murmured the Captain.

"Four years ago, right here at the Tunbridge Fair, I had a few beers in this beer hall—that's why the press conference is here, for those of you interested in cosmic significance—with a woman who wasn't my wife. One thing led to another, and we ended up you-know-whating out in the parking lot. Then later I lied about it to my wife, to her husband, and to the people of Central Vermont."

There was more silence. Glances were being exchanged like handshakes at a convention. Finally Benny Malone spoke:

"Darwin, was this woman the Queen of England or Cher or somebody?"

"No," said Darwin somberly, "she's local."

"So let me get this straight," said Cilly Dupras, pencil poised to write on a still-blank note pad, "Four years ago you came to the Tunbridge Fair, screwed some lady, then later on lied about it."

Darwin fidgeted and cleared his throat before booming, "That's absolutely right!"

The Associated Press bureau chief from Montpelier was next: "Am I missing something? What is the newsworthy element of this event?" The remark set off a torrent from the floor.

"Tunbridge Fair doesn't count."

"Happens hundreds of times each fair. Think I'm going to write that?"

"Fifth of liquor and another man's wife."

"Tunbridge Fair is a freebie."

"Where's Fenvessey, he's the one who dragged us here."

"Let's hustle up to the ox pull and get some shots of some rural shit. My editor will kill me if I come back empty-handed."

Notebooks slammed shut, cameras were tucked under arms, and a motley, disgusted press corps exited. Only Gimp stayed behind with Billy and Darwin.

"Darwin, you said this was a blockbuster. Those guys will be ragging on me for years."

"I thought it was, Gimp. You know: 'Total Disclosure Guy a Fraud.' If the press made such a big deal out of Total Disclosure the first time around, I thought this would be of interest."

Gimp shook his head. "Darwin, you don't understand the media. They use things up. Shoot yourself on national TV. Hijack a Greyhound bus and drive it to Cuba. These things are nice little blips in a business that has to find a new way to stimulate its audience every twenty-four hours. You rode the crest pretty well, but they used you up too. You're of as much interest as last season's baseball scores.

"But what really mystifies me is that you don't understand about the Tunbridge Fair either. This is the Vermonters last gasp at life before the bleak season. Any reporter whose byline appeared under a story exposing the Tunbridge Fair better make himself scarce come deer season. You know all this."

"I've always loved the Fair. I guess the species needs an occasional vehicle for releasing steam."

"Needs it? If the Tunbridge Fair didn't exist, they would have to invent it real fast! After the fair we face one very long, cold winter. And it's not just the horny who need the fair. Kids, old folks, farmers—there's something for everyone here."

"Gimp, I know everything you're telling me. I guess I've been so preoccupied that I need to look at things through fresh eyes."

Darwin wandered the fair with the Captain. The day was brilliant, inspirational.

"Now, this is a beautiful morning," said Billy Mann.

"Reminds me of a tune," interrupted Darwin.

"Young Rascals, 1971," said the Captain, not about to be upstaged where music was concerned. "Felix Cavaliere on vocals. We get about a dozen perfect days a year."

"Is it really over?" Darwin needed reassurance.

"Nothing's over. Election Day is seven weeks of ball-busting work away."

"You know what I mean. Someone has waved a magic wand, and without anything changing, everything's changed."

"He really does have the whole world in his hands." The Captain smiled. "But let's not forget, we're here to work." He pulled out a placard bordered with DAIRYMEN FOR DARWIN bumper stickers with a neatly hand-inscribed message, MEET THE CANDIDATE. Both men stuffed their pockets with handout brochures. They looked at each other, shook hands, and set out to face the world.

They meandered through the Exhibition Hall, watched the contra dancers, ate French fries with salt and vinegar,

213

and watched fluffy sheep compete for blue ribbons. The crowd swelled as the day went on.

"Howyadoin'," said Darwin to each new face with which he could make contact. "My name's Darwin, and I need your vote. What do you think the most important issues are?"

Sunny came with the three kids right after school let out, and Darwin repeated the same circuit as earlier, experiencing the Fair again through the fresh eyes of his children, and without the paraphernalia of a politician. Most of Central Vermont was in attendance, and Darwin reveled in the constant acquaintance that was an integral part of the Tunbridge experience. Among those in attendance were the competition.

Linwood "Woody" Dunwoody was wearing a suit and working the midway. His backslapping guffaws outdecibeled even the loudest barkers. When he saw Darwin, he challenged him to a contest of strength with the mallet to see who could ring the bell.

Darwin good-naturedly took the hammer and gave it his all. Three times he swung, three times he lifted the steel marker to the Fooling Around mark.

"Seems appropriate to me," he said, handing the mallet to Dunwoody.

Dunwoody smirked. "You swing like a Flatlander." The crowd of seventy roared. He swung three times, his body a study in timing and grace. The bell rang clearly each time.

"Winner and still cham-peen!" declared Dunwoody, his arms thrust skyward in victory.

"Yup," agreed Darwin. "You're Chuck of the Universe, all right. Care to go a few laps around the track?"

"Only if Weinstein will join us," he boomed. "But her high heels might get stuck in the mud."

Dunwoody et al dissolved in hilarity. Women and Flatlanders were always in season. Darwin left sharing their mirth, earning at least a few points for sportsmanship.

The neighbors were there as well. Joe and Tina Pisano were a bit frantic. Their children had entries in craft projects, exotic poultry, and vegetable composites. One hour before the judging, their prize Dutch-miniature lop-earred rabbit had given birth to a dozen pink slugs.

"This isn't funny," snapped Joe, seeing Darwin smile as he related the story.

"Yes, it is," interjected Tina. Suddenly they were all laughing.

Darwin Jr. and Olin Blanchard collided in the Moonwalk, an inflatable trampoline for kids, and Olin got a nosebleed of middling proportions.

"Sniff it in," commanded Bennett. Darwin went for his handkerchief and began dabbing.

"I'm the nurturing type," he explained. "Where's Teresa?"

"Passing out leaflets for you," snapped Bennett.

"Oh." Darwin looked for a change in subject. "How's your Dad?"

"Tougher'n a goat. Cain't wait to get back to work."

"Must be extra work for you."

Bennett shrugged. These shoulders are meant for work, he seemed to say. The gesture sufficed as an answer, but Bennett had a last comment: "I'll be glad when you're elected senator and life can return to normal."

Emil Dummerston Weed, who had the day shift at the volunteer fire department's French fry booth, took Sunny off Darwin's hands.

"Your timing is impeccable," said Darwin. "In the last two hours she has consumed, perhaps I should say 'powered down,' two corn dogs, one piece of pepperoni pizza, a candy apple, an Italian sausage with peppers and onions, a grilled turkey leg, and two salads in a pocket."

Emil beamed at his betrothed: "I'm proud of you, darlin'. Not only have you single-handedly assured the prosperity of the Fair's concessionaires, you've saved me from spendin' a cent."

"All's I did was chow down before you got me, just like you said."

"Good girl," said Emil, " 'cuz all you'll get outta me is beer."

"And all I'll get out of that food is a zit face so ugly it'd make a train take a dirt road."

Emil snickered pridefully, and Sunny leaned her head on his shoulder in adoration. This union, thought Darwin, is made in heaven.

Hannah Duncan and Howard "Warren" Pease were observed together on the merry-go-round. He was discoursing on mechanical amusements, their history, their construction, their economic payback. She looked as if she were evaluating her odds of survival if she climbed out of the cab and scaled down the superstructure to terra firma.

Natalie Weinstein worked the crowd near the pavilion where the Divinity Fudge was sold. Sammi was at her side, passing out WOMEN FOR WEINSTEIN bumper stickers to everyone who stopped to shake the candidate's hand. She bypassed Darwin and went straight to the children, leaving the two candidates to make small talk.

"She's not coming back," reasserted Weinstein.

"I hope you're wrong," returned Darwin.

"Are you working the beer hall tonight?" she asked.

Darwin took in a slow breath. He rolled his eyes and made an audible groan. "I'll tell you a long story about that someday," he said.

Butcher Barnham and family were sharing—make that devouring—a humongous order of onion rings. Darwin was so caught up in the spirit of the Fair that he considered going over to say hello, but thought better of it and turned the other way. They seemed to be having such a good time; it was not his place to ruin it.

Riley Gore was the master of ceremonies for the evening show of country and western music. He passed Darwin on the midway. Darwin greeted him with a spontaneous "Gray Fox!" But Gore waved perfunctorily and brushed by, his eyes registering not a flicker of recognition, just the weariness of coping with fame.

The biggest surprise was Sue Clarke, wandering through the livestock barns. It had been more than a month since she left town, and now she greeted Darwin, never her closest friend, with a warm hug of reunion and a wet kiss on the lips.

"Where's my husband?" she asked after unsmacking.

"If he's like the rest of the world, he's around here someplace. Are you back for good?"

"Yes," she said emphatically, then gave Darwin another hug. "Oh Darwin, I'm so glad to be back. I was lying in a fancy hotel in Palos Verdes. I'd been following the Celtics during exhibition season, pandering to these oversized, spoiled children, playing meaningless game after meaningless game. Then Stevie came in to tell me he'd been cut from the team. In no time at all he's packing his bags to return home to Terre Haute, Indiana, to marry the girl next door and to become assistant sales manager and chief figurehead at his uncle's Hyundai dealership. Suddenly I missed the real world! Can I walk with you for a while?"

Darwin said sure. Within an hour they encountered Townshend and Walt up by the display of antique farm implements. Townshend was shocked to see Sue, but even more shocked to be the recipient of her fond caresses. The kids actually had to wait their turn, even Heather, whose arm was now as good as new. Townshend had abandoned his shaved head, and his shaved face, as well. Two week's growth was everywhere.

"Townshend," said Darwin, "you look as if someone dipped your head in a vat of hair."

"We've got the hottest idea ever," Townshend squeaked out between kisses.

Walt picked up the speech: "This is even better than 1839. We're going to take the land we acquired for the development and put it into Christmas trees. Do you know what they get for Christmas trees in Manhattan? Seventy-five bucks!"

"Perfect," said Darwin. "It's a dynamite idea. Perfect, perfect, perfect, perfect."

The month after the Tunbridge World's Fair was the busiest of Darwin's life. He caught up on his patients, campaigned until the wee hours (which in Vermont commence at nine P.M.), and snatched sleep when he could. He lusted for feedback. The final report card would come in a few weeks, but he needed something to keep him going.

Howard "Warren" Pease came to his rescue. He promised, in an unobtrusive, Vermont kind of way, to survey the people who came into his store as to their awareness and inclination concerning the upcoming elections. Then he would tabulate results and project the outcome with the assistance of his trusty Macintosh SE. With less than a week before the election, Darwin stopped in for an update.

"How'm I doin'?"

"You sound terrible," said Warren.

"I gotta code. My head feels like it's stupped wid coddon. Whud's da compudah say?"

"It's very interesting," started Warren. Darwin braced himself for tedium. "The race appears to be neck and neck and neck. Everyone is aware of it. Everyone has an opinion. Everyone is going to vote. And goddamn if I can tell who's leading right now. I will say that you are a bona fide candidate, Darwin. Among your attributes, people cite your 'kick butt' attitude—fifty-two-percent approval rating—Total Disclosure, forty-seven percent, the fact that you saved that old lady—sixty-one percent—and the fact that you worked Friday during the day at Tunbridge Fair, thirty-nine percent. Do you want to know what they don't like about you?"

"Spare me."

"Okay. Want me to bring anything tonight?"

"Fuh whut?"

"Your Halloween party. Sunny invited me last week. My costume is all prepared."

"Terrifuk. Come on up, but dif yer gonna brin' sumpin', brin' sumpin for dis cold."

Darwin had the autumn crud. This virus of unspecified origin runs roughshod through the Northland as soon as the weather turns nasty. It originates in elementary schools

219

and spirals outward until everyone in the Northland is coughing, sneezing, and feeling clear-headed as horseshoe crabs.

Darwin caught the bug from Duke, who caught it from Jennifer Clarke, who caught it from Amy, who caught it from Darwin Jr., who caught it from Bobby Pisano, ad infinitum. Darwin was not interested in the virus's family tree so much as a cure, however temporary. He had survived appointments with patients and a meeting with the Hopping Housewives of Greater Granville. But he had forgotten about Halloween.

He had taken four Contac cold capsules, twelve aspirin, and Afrin nasal spray. He estimated his IQ at less than sixty.

The Hunter household was the traditional headquarters for festivities. "Whud's da progr'm?" he asked Sunny as soon as he came through the door.

"You sound like death. You sound wors'n my uncle right before he died. Everyone's invited to a bonfire for a drink; then the kids will go trick or treating. They'll be coming in a half hour."

"Thad's simble 'nough."

"I told everyone to come in costume."

"Fine, whud'r you goin' t'be?"

"Nancy Nixon."

"Who's Nanthy Nixthon?"

"You know. The President's wife?"

"Oh, right." Darwin considered correcting her, but knew he'd have as much success talking General Beauregard into becoming a dalmatian. "I tink I'll be rilly creative—wrappa towel aroun' my head'n say I'ma pirate."

"With all that hacking and nose blowing you're doing, you could go as Rudolph the Red-Nosed Reindeer." Darwin was struck by the fact that despite deep roots in Vermont Chuckdom, Sunny had developed a sense of humor much like his wife's. It was to be his last coherent thought of the night.

"I'm going to make you a tonic!" Sunny said with gusto, bottles and pans already clanking.

"How 'bout some dinnuh?"

"No time. You have to get in your costume and start the bonfire."

Darwin opted for a beer to satisfy his empty stomach, and set out listlessly to transform himself into a swashbuckling pirate. He was putting on a gold earring when Sunny burst into his bedroom with a cupful of steaming brown liquid.

"Drink this," she commanded. "My Daddy swears by it. Drink it all at once."

Darwin obeyed and nearly choked. His throat and gut burned, forcing him to his beer for relief. "What's that?" he gasped. Actually, "Whuzdat?"

She spewed off the recipe, but he lost interest after the fruit pectin, bourbon, and cayenne pepper.

Darwin managed to start the bonfire. Wherever he stood, the smoke was drawn to him, making his already bleary eyes burn. Hannah Duncan arrived dressed as Scarlett O'Hara. Her costume was so elaborate, her makeup so complete, and the light so dim, that Darwin didn't recognize her.

"I can't bleevit," he murmured after she revealed her identity, "I can't bleevit."

At seven the community descended on the fire. Children dressed as ballerinas, ghouls, Michael Jacksons, and Supermen flitted like noisy sparks. The decibel level alone ensured chaos. A walking mass of foliage approached:

"Hey, Darwin, c'mere. I can't get too close to the flame."
The voice was vaguely familiar. Darwin pushed his numb
brain to comprehend.

"Who are you?"

"I'm a politician just like you. Don't you recognize me?
I'm George Bush. Here, you need a drink of cider." The
figure extended a quart mason jar toward him. Darwin
was parched from the antihistamines he had been taking,
and took a generous swallow. The liquid went down his
throat like a load of fiery gravel.

"Whud's that?" he choked out.

"Applejack." He now recognized the voice. The man
behind the bush was Gimp.

"Mus'be a hundred 'n' twenty proof."

"A hundred fifty, near as we can guess. It will cure what
ails ya."

"By killing you," Darwin pointed out. The vapors of the
alcohol stimulated his sinuses momentarily, then left him
feeling like the headless horseman. For the rest of the
evening Darwin carried his beleaguered head underneath
his arm.

The darkness, the smoke, the applejack, the antihistamines, the cold, the campaign—Darwin's mental capabil-
ities receded to the Paleolithic era. His words slurred; his
movements slowed to a creep. He was conducting his life
in a world of molasses.

He spoke to people he could not recognize. There was
a country and western singer, a human bowling ball, and
the wife of a President. These were his friends and neighbors, but he recognized no one. At the fire three cackling
witches stirred a caldron. He pushed his mind to see who
they were, but the makeup was too effective. He moved
closer. They were chanting in verse, punctuating the

rhythms with shrieks. He swore one of them added a live rat to the potion. Another held out a ladle. Here, Darwin. Drink this. Mimi Cox! And the other two—Natalie Weinstein and Teresa Blanchard. Something was seriously wrong here. This did not compute.

Darwin backed up directly into someone. He turned to see the weathered creases of Linwood "Woody" Dunwoody's face booming out a laugh. Then Dunwoody handed him another glass of applejack and challenged him to a chugging contest, winner takes all. Darwin obliged, chugged, lost. But it turned out not to be Dunwoody at all; it was Townshend Clarke, dressed as Dunwoody.

Darwin sought a point of reference. There was none. He considered lying down next to the fire and drifting off to sleep. The idea was beguiling. Finally, there was a voice in the distance calling his name. It came closer and closer. He realized the voice was no more than a foot behind him. He mustered all his resources to turn:

"Darwin, you look terrible. Let me put you to bed."

It was his wife, Sammi Berger-Hunter, dressed as a fairy godmother, infused with the milk of human kindness:

"I'm coming home, Darwin," her words had the soothing coolness of morning dew. "I'm here, and I'm here for good."

"You don' whadda catch dis code," he blurted through thickened lips.

"I'll catch whatever I want," she said, taking his arm. "Your germs are my germs."

During the night his fever broke amid vivid dreams of witches by firelight. (It must have been the applejack.) He was well enough to go to work and to stumble through his campaign duties. And Sammi really was home. She was by his side when he awoke. She cooked his breakfast. She was there when he returned at night. Aside from the fact that she was still actively working for the Weinstein campaign, she was every bit the devoted wife.

"Are you back to stay?" he asked.

"Yes. I think so. Let's put it this way, I'll disappoint myself if I change my mind."

"You used the first person four times in that last statement."

Sammi laughed. "I've just come through a period of intense self-examination." Her manner was more relaxed than Darwin remembered.

"What did you learn?"

"Oh, little bits and pieces, like about priorities, and investment, and passion. There was no grand moment when I screamed 'AHA, I've seen the error of my ways!' And really, nothing has changed. The problems haven't disappeared. The difference is that they don't seem as important as when I left. And the other difference is that I no longer hold you singularly responsible for my happiness."

Darwin studied the grounds in the bottom of his coffee cup. He tried hard to keep the dink out his voice. "Are you still seeking a multigamous relationship?"

" 'Mul-tig-a-muss'? What magazine did you get that out of?" They both smiled. "No, Darwin, I promise to love, obey, and cherish you."

"Well, let's not overdo it. You don't even have to vote for me."

"Don't worry, I won't."

"So is this a good marriage?"

"Any marriage that bounces back is good."

"By the way," asked Darwin, "who were those witches last night?"

"There were no witches," she replied.

Darwin ran on adrenaline now, the final countdown to Election Day. He attended every meeting that would have him, worked the bars and grocery store checkouts, spent his Saturdays shaking hands at the sanitary landfill. It was going well, he told himself. Sammi's home, and I'm doing the best I can.

When he came home for dinner on the Monday before Election Day, he announced to the family that it was over. He had done as much as he could, and whatever the outcome, he was satisfied that he'd given it his best shot. General Beauregard thumped his approval, the kids were distracted by a mayonnaise commercial on TV, and Sammi asked him to repeat himself, since she could not hear above the noise from the Jenn-Aire kitchen range.

After dinner Darwin went to visit Hoyt Blanchard, as he had several times throughout the fall. He knew at seven-thirty Stella would be tending to the dinner dishes, and Hoyt would have settled into his La-Z-Boy recliner to watch the nighttime version of *Hollywood Squares*.

Darwin had said nothing of his trip to New Bedford. Tonight he simply handed the china cup to the old farmer and waited for the flicker of recognition before speaking:

"I saw her, Hoyt, your 'Quita. She's beautiful now, just as she was when you were with her. And she's well. She's had a good life, just like you, filled with fond memories and no regrets. She sent you this cup. You can keep it out in the barn and think of her every time you take a sip of milk or water. Both of you can rest easy that you did the right thing."

There was too much emotion for Hoyt to muster words. The television blared with crude comments from Joan Rivers and an audience perpetually on the verge of hysterical pandemonium. But even a marching band could not ripple the peaceful calm of the Blanchard parlor in Upper Granville, Vermont. Stella entered, made a small fuss over Darwin's presence and the impending election, and offered tea, which Darwin declined. Then she returned to the kitchen. Darwin stood to leave, knowing there was still a question to be answered.

"Did she have my child?"

"No, Hoyt. You were right. She was pregnant, but she lost the baby. Eventually she had children, but not yours. It wasn't meant to be."

"Is this the truth, Darwin?"

Darwin nodded. "If there's one thing I've learned about these past few months, it's about telling the truth."

Emil Dummerston Weed knocked at the Hunter door, but the household was still asleep, not surprising for five-thirty in the morning. The kitchen door was unlocked, so Emil entered and repeated his rapping on Darwin and Sammi's bedroom door:

"Let's go, partner. Up and at 'em. You know what day today is, don't you?"

Darwin emerged slowly, thickly, slumber still in his eyes. "I know what today is. What I don't know is, why does Emil Dummerston Weed find it necessary to break into our house at five-thirty in the morning to tell me that it's Election Day?"

"I fergot about Election Day. I'm talking Pig Slaughterin' Day. We're takin' them porkers to make 'em into wieners. I'll put on some water for coffee."

"How very appropriate," mused Darwin, warming to the idea. "What a monumental pain in the ass, but entirely appropriate."

"Don't wear your good clothes," shouted Emil. "We're gonna be doin' some rasslin'."

Darwin was exhausted, yet exhilarated by the time he arrived at the Granville Elementary School an hour before the polls opened. He was bruised and sore, having gone his ten rounds with pigs named Dunwoody and Weinstein, but filled with the sweet wine of victory. Billy Mann was waiting for him, having staked out the best turf for Darwin to greet the voting public. Soon they were joined by Natalie Weinstein, then later, a confident Dunwoody and entourage.

Sammi arrived separately and joined forces with Weinstein.

"I may love you, Darwin, but I can't bring myself to vote for you."

"Still too much of a dink?"

"Yes, but now I think of you fondly as King Dink." She punctuated it with a kiss on the cheek.

A woman came out and informed the candidates that the polls were now opening and that the candidates would be allowed to cast the first votes.

"This is it," Darwin told the Captain. "The thousands of handshakes, the miles of smiles—it all comes down to this."

"How do you feel?" the Captain asked.

"Like the luckiest man in the world. I feel invincible," said Darwin, shadow boxing an imaginary Marvin Hagler. "I feel like kicking butt."

Darwin was the first to cast his vote. Before entering the booth he paused to shake the hands of his opponents one last time.

"May the best man win," he said to Weinstein.

"Darwin"—she held his hand—"she may be back, but it won't last. Take care of yourself, will you?"

He swallowed hard and tried to return her direct stare. He moved on to Dunwoody. "It's been a helluva horse race," he said.

"You did a lot better than I thought," answered Dunwoody.

"Only in America—" began Darwin, but Dunwoody cut him off.

"Can a fool with no idea how the system works run for elective office!"

Dunwoody was good-natured, loud, and gregarious, as usual. He squeezed Darwin's hand unnecessarily hard. There was no sentiment, however, only territorial posturing. Darwin held his ground and completed the statement, with a confident smile:

"And win by a landslide."

His campaign over, he turned to vote.